PUFFIN BOOKS

THE THREE PRINCES OF PERSIA

Rohini Chowdhury was born in Kolkata and educated at Loreto House, Jadavpur University, and IIM, Ahmedabad. She has written several books for children. She also runs a story website for children www.longlongtimeago.com.

She now lives behind a keyboard in London, with her one husband, two daughters, a herb garden and no pets.

The Three Princes of Persia

Children in World Myth

ROHINI CHOWDHURY

Illustrated by

VISHWAJYOTI GHOSH

PUFFIN BOOKS

PUFFIN
Published by the Penguin Group
Penguin Books India Pvt Ltd, 11 Community Centre, Panchsheel Park, New Delhi 110 017, India
Penguin Group (USA) Inc., 375 Hudson Street, New York, New York 10014, USA
Penguin Group (Canada), 10 Alcorn Avenue, Toronto, Ontario, Canada M4V 3B2 (a division of Pearson Penguin Canada Inc.)
Penguin Books Ltd, 80 Strand, London WC2R 0RL, England
Penguin Ireland, 25 St Stephen's Green, Dublin 2, Ireland (a division of Penguin Books Ltd)
Penguin Group (Australia), 250 Camberwell Road, Camberwell, Victoria 3124, Australia (a division of Pearson Australia Group Pty Ltd)
Penguin Group (NZ), cnr Airborne and Rosedale Roads, Albany, Auckland 1310, New Zealand (a division of Pearson New Zealand Ltd)
Penguin Group (South Africa) (Pty) Ltd, 24 Sturdee Avenue, Rosebank, Johannesburg 2196, South Africa

Penguin Books Ltd, Registered Offices: 80 Strand, London WC2R 0RL, England

First published by Penguin Books India 2005

10 9 8 7 6 5 4 3 2 1

Typeset by Eleven Arts, New Delhi
Printed at Pauls Press, New Delhi

In memory of Ma,
who gave me stories
and so much else,
And to my mother,
who listened to these tales.

Contents

Acknowledgements

I would like to thank Usha Bubna, Piyali Sengupta and Urmi Sen for their unflagging support and encouragement. They were my critics, my research team, and remarkably, my friends right through. I am also extremely grateful to my editor Sayoni Basu, for her patience and for her understanding of what I wished to achieve with this collection. Last, but not least, my gratitude and thanks to my husband Atul Bansal, and my daughters Vipasha and Vidisha, who put up with me cheerfully right through the making of this book.

The Three Princes of Persia

The *Shah Namah* or the *Book of Kings* is an epic poem composed by the celebrated Persian poet Firdausi. Completed in AD 1010, the epic is written in Pahlavi and consists of 60,000 verses which took Firdausi thirty-five years to compose. Firdausi presented the poem to the famous sultan, Mahmud Ghaznavi, who by that time had become ruler of Firdausi's homeland, Khurasan.

The *Shah Namah* is based mainly on the *Khvatay-Namak*, a history of the kings of Persia (the ancient name for Iran) from mythical times to the beginning of the seventh century AD. Firdausi extended the poem to include events up to the mid-seventh century. The epic remains one of the most popular works in the Persian-speaking world even today.

One of the stories contained in the *Shah Namah* is that of

Rustam, Persia's greatest hero. Firdausi writes of the childhood of Rustam and of his long, full life. He tells also of Rustam's great deeds of bravery and heroism, of his love for Princess Tahminah, and of their son Sohrab.

Three tales from the *Shah Namah* are retold here—that of the birth and childhood of Zal, Rustam's father; of the boyhood of Rustam himself; and that of Sohrab's short life and tragic death.

Zal the White-Haired

Long ago, in the land of Seistan, which lies to the south of the country we call Iran, there ruled the Pahlavi chieftain Saum. Saum was a just and powerful ruler, and under him the land was happy. Saum too was happy and lacked for nothing—except a child. His great grief was that he had no child of his own.

Then one day a son was born to him. The child was perfect in every way and as beautiful and radiant as the moon—except that his hair was as white as that of an old man. When the women saw this beautiful baby, but with hair as white as that of an old man, they were afraid to tell Saum in case he was angry at this strange feature of his son. Thus eight days passed after the birth of the child before one of the women plucked up enough courage to go to Saum with the news.

Bowing low before the great chieftain, the woman begged leave to speak. 'May the days of Saum the hero be happy, for a son has been born to him!' cried the woman. 'The child is beautiful, and without fault or blemish, except that his hair is as white as that of an aged man. But I beg you, O Saum my master, to look upon this child as a divine gift, and not be angry at his one fault.'

Saum heard the woman in silence, and when she had finished, rose and went into the women's quarters where lay his baby son. Saum looked at the child, so perfect in every way, except for his white hair. Forgetting all his wisdom, Saum thought, 'Will not my enemies laugh at me for this strange-looking son? Will they not say he is an omen of evil? How will I answer them?' Saum railed against Fate who had been so unkind to him, and in his anger cried to the servants, 'Take this blemish upon Persia and throw him out of the land!'

The servants did as their master commanded. Far, far away, where no men live, there stands a mountain, Elburz, whose head touches the stars. No mortal man has ever scaled this peak, nor ever will. At the foot of this mountain, where grown men are afraid to venture, the servants of Saum laid their master's infant son and left him to die. There, the Simurgh saw him.

The Simurgh is a giant bird, with the feathers of a peacock, the wings of an eagle, the head of a dog and the claws of a lion. She is so old that she has seen the world destroyed three times over, and so wise that she holds within her the knowledge of all ages. Upon the crest of Elburz, the Simurgh had her nest—a nest built of ebony and sandalwood and twined about with herbs and healing plants so that no evil could come near it. In the nest were the Simurgh's chicks, her little ones that she cared for as tenderly as any mother.

When the Simurgh saw the little baby, abandoned at the foot of Elburz, uncared for, unwanted, without clothes to keep him warm and sucking his fingers with hunger, she thought he'd make a good meal for her chicks. So down she swooped from the mountain crest, and snatching up the baby in her talons carried him up to her nest. But she did not feed him to her chicks—her mother's heart went out to the helpless baby, and she decided to bring him up with her own brood. 'Do not harm this human child, but treat him like a brother,' the Simurgh told her chicks. She covered the baby with her feathers for warmth, and gently fed him tender bits of meat so that he would no longer be hungry.

The Simurgh loved and cherished the baby like her own, and never wearied of looking after him. In this way, many years passed, and the baby grew up into a tall and handsome youth. Slowly the people of the land became aware of this young and handsome man who lived upon the crest of Elburz, and stories about him spread far and wide, till finally they reached the ears of Saum.

Then one night Saum had a strange dream. He dreamt that a man came riding towards him with news of his son, and then mocked him, saying, 'Oh, you most unhappy man, who disowned your son because his hair was white, even though your own is silver! You, who have left your son in the care of a bird all his life, and have forsaken all the duties of fatherhood! Do you intend to disregard your son forever?'

Saum awoke, deeply distressed. He called the wise men of his kingdom together and asked them the meaning of his dream. 'Can it be that my son is still alive?' he said. 'Would he not have died of cold and hunger yet?'

And the wise men answered him, 'Oh, you most unhappy man, your son is still alive. You are more cruel than the lion, more unfeeling than the tiger and the crocodile! For even wild animals care for their young—while you abandoned your son and left him to die only because his hair was white! Go now, and seek your son—and pray that he forgives you!'

When Saum heard this he was overcome with remorse. Calling his army together, he set off for Mount Elburz. There, upon its crest, he saw the Simurgh and her nest, and a young man who looked like himself. Saum began to climb, slowly and laboriously, up the side of Elburz—but try as he might, he could not reach the top. Desperate to reach his son, Saum fell to his knees at the foot of Elburz—there was about him no arrogance, no pride and no anger—only remorse at what he had done, and great love for his son.

Just then the Simurgh looked down, and saw Saum kneeling at the foot of Elburz. The great bird knew why he had come. She turned to the boy she had brought up as her own and said to him, 'Oh, my dear one, whom I have loved as my own, the hour of our parting has come. Saum, greatest of all heroes, your father, awaits you at the foot of this mountain. Go to him, for a great future is there for you as Saum's beloved son.'

The boy looked at the great bird who had been both mother and father to him. Tears filled his eyes, and he said to the Simurgh, 'Why do you send me away? Are you tired of me? Your nest is more to me than a palace or a throne, your wings are all the love I ever need. You gave me shelter when my father abandoned me. Why do you now send me to him?'

But the Simurgh answered, 'I do not send you away because I do not love you, my son. If I could I would keep you with me forever. But a great destiny awaits you. Go out into the world therefore, and try your fortune.' Then, plucking out a feather from her breast and giving it to the boy, the Simurgh said, 'Take this feather with you to remember me by. If you are ever in trouble, throw this feather into the fire, and I will come to your aid.' And holding the boy in her talons, the Simurgh carried him gently down to Saum.

Saum, when he saw the great Simurgh, bowed low in front of her, and wept out his gratitude for all that she had done. As the Simurgh flew back up to her nest on Elburz, Saum had eyes only for his son. He saw a tall and handsome boy, young, strong and intelligent and perfect in every way, save for his silver hair. Saum's heart swelled with pride in his son and love for him. He hugged him and begged his forgiveness and promised that never again would he turn away from him.

Saum then dressed his son in rich robes, and named him 'Zal' which means 'aged'. Saum's army welcomed Zal with cheers and shouts of happiness, for never had they seen so handsome and strong a youth. Then Saum and his army turned back towards Seistan, taking Zal with them. The news spread before them that Saum had found his son, who was a hero among men, and the land was filled with joy and celebration.

Thus Saum found his son again, and Zal the White-Haired came back to Seistan to his father's home. Zal was taught the art of kingship and grew to be a great hero, and a just and wise ruler.

Rustam the Valiant

To Zal the White-Haired and his lovely bride Rudabeh was born a beautiful baby boy, whom they called Rustam. Rustam was a strong and healthy baby, perfect in every way. When the people of Seistan heard that a son had been born to their prince, they broke into a frenzy of happiness and joy, and the sound of feasting and dancing resounded throughout the land.

At this time, Saum the mighty hero, father of Zal and grandfather to the baby Rustam, was away from his country, fighting to protect the borders of Persia. So Zal sent messengers to Saum to tell him of the birth of his grandson and carrying with them a portrait of the baby embroidered in fine silk.

Saum received the messengers joyfully and showered them with gold, and thought himself fortunate that he would be able to see his grandson's face one day. But it was to be eight long years before Saum returned home and finally saw Rustam.

As Saum and his army approached his country, they saw a mighty procession riding out to greet them. At the head was a huge elephant, richly caparisoned, and riding high upon it a boy of eight. Saum's heart leapt for joy when he saw the child, for he knew that this was no other than Rustam, his beloved grandchild.

Rustam climbed down from the great elephant, and bowing low to the ground, greeted his grandfather with great respect. Saum embraced Rustam and held him close, and made him ride beside him. And so the two rode into the city together where cheering crowds lined the streets to welcome home their chieftain.

Rustam had grown into a tall, handsome and clever little boy. Saum spent all his time with his grandson, telling him of his campaigns and battles, and listening to what he had to say. Rustam was intelligent, thoughtful and sensible, as well as strong and handsome.

'Oh, Grandfather,' said Rustam one day to Saum. 'I am happy that I am your grandson, for it is like you that I wish to be. I find no joy in feasting or toys, nor am I looking for a life of ease and rest. All that I want is a horse of my own, armour and arrows and a shield. I want to ride into battle the way you do, and to fight all our enemies, every one, till the last of them lies defeated in the sand.'

Saum heard his little grandson speak so seriously of such matters with astonishment, and then with growing joy. 'Truly, this child will do great deeds,' thought Saum to himself, and blessed the boy.

At last, after a month, it became necessary once again for Saum to return to the battlefield. Before he left, he took his son Zal aside and said, 'My son, one parting favour I ask of you. When Rustam your son, my grandchild, is as tall as you, let him choose a horse for himself, and the weapons that he desires. Do this, for my sake, and in my honour.' Zal promised to do as his father asked, and soon Saum left for the battlefield again.

Rustam continued to grow in strength and wisdom under the care of his mother and the wise guidance of his father. Almost two years passed since Saum's visit, and Rustam was now almost ten years old.

One night, Rustam was woken from a peaceful sleep by a great rumbling and roaring. Rustam sat up in bed and wondered what it could be. Outside the closed door of his room he could hear the sound of people running and screaming and shouting as though in fear of their lives.

'What is it? What is happening?' called Rustam. His servants, shaking with fright, answered that the Shah's white elephant had gone mad and broken its chains, and the people in the palace were in danger.

Rustam jumped out of bed and ordered the guards to let him out so that he may subdue the animal. But the guards barred his way. 'What will we say to the Shah if you run into danger?' they cried. 'We cannot let you, a mere boy, go out to face that giant elephant!'

But Rustam would not listen. He forced a way through the guards, and breaking down the door, ran out into the courtyard. There stood the huge white elephant, mad with rage. The warriors and soldiers stood huddled in a corner, terrified of the great animal, and unable to do a thing to stop its madness.

Rustam ran towards the elephant. The elephant saw the boy, and trumpeting furiously, charged at him with its trunk raised, its eyes gleaming with madness. Rustam stood his ground without flinching, and raising his club, struck the elephant on its head, so that it fell down dead. Satisfied that the animal was really dead and no longer a danger, Rustam returned to his room and went to bed, and slept peacefully till morning.

But the story of his heroic deed flew through the city and the whole of the land. The people rejoiced that once again a hero had risen in Persia.

Soon after this it happened that Minuchihir, the good and wise Shah of Persia, died. Civil war broke out in the land, as rival factions tried to capture the throne. In the middle of this strife, and while trying to bring peace to the land and ensure the accession of the rightful heir to the throne of Persia, Saum died as well. Zal was plunged into grief, and mourned his father greatly. Seeing that the mighty Saum was dead, and that Zal too was overcome with grief, the enemies of the rightful successor to Minuchihir grew bolder and the war increased in intensity.

The people of Persia turned to Zal, and first blamed him for their sorrow and then begged him to save their land. Then Zal spoke to them and said, 'I have always done what is right for my people and for the land of Persia. I have feared no enemy except old age. But sadly, that enemy is now with me, for I have grown too old to go into battle. But I give to you Rustam my son. He is only a boy, but he has the signs of greatness about him. And what's more, he shall be supported by all my wisdom and experience, for I shall be ever available to advise and guide him.' The people of Persia bowed their heads and accepted with gratitude Rustam as their leader.

Then Zal called Rustam to him and said, 'My son, you are still so young. But Persia has need of you, and I must send you out to face its enemies, warriors of great prowess and skill.'

Rustam saw that his father was troubled. He smiled and said to him, 'Oh, Father, you know that I take no pleasure in the games that children play. All I want is to go to war. So give to me the mace of Saum, your father, and let me choose a horse of my own liking. Then let me go to war, so that I may vanquish our enemies, and bring peace to our land again.'

Rustam's brave words reassured Zal. Honouring Saum's

parting request that Rustam be allowed to choose his own horse when the time came, and respecting the boy's own wishes as well, Zal ordered that all the finest horses in the land be brought before Rustam. The word went out that Rustam, son of Zal, was choosing his horse, and men came from far and wide bringing their herds with them.

One by one the finest horses in the land were paraded in front of the boy. Rustam looked at each, and as they passed before him, placed his hand on their backs to see if they could bear his weight. But every horse that he so tested sank shuddering to the ground before him—till he came to the herds of Kabul.

Among the herds of Kabul, Rustam saw a mare tall and strong. And behind her, there followed a colt, high-spirited and strong, and its colour was that of rose leaves scattered on a saffron background. Rustam liked the colt, and snared it neatly, pulling it out of the herd. The mare fought to protect her colt, but Rustam's will prevailed.

The keeper of the herd saw Rustam and, not recognizing him, came running up to warn him not to take the colt, for it belonged to someone else. 'Whom does it belong to?' asked Rustam. 'I do not see its owner's mark upon the animal.'

'We do not know his master,' said the keeper. 'But it has been said that this colt belongs to Rustam. Its mother does not allow any man to ride it. For three years now it has been ready to wear a saddle, but no man has been able to tame it.'

When Rustam heard this, he swung himself on to the colt's back in a single bound. The mare came charging, as though she would knock Rustam off, but when he spoke to her, she calmed down. And the rose-coloured colt flew across the plain, with Rustam on its back, as easily as the wind.

When Rustam returned, he said to the keeper, 'What price do you want for this marvellous animal?'

The keeper answered, 'If you are Rustam, then take it, and mounted on its back, deliver Persia from strife and war. Its price is the land of Persia, and seated upon it, you will save the world.'

So Rustam took the colt, which was named Rakush, meaning 'Lightning'. Then Zal and Rustam prepared to take their stand against the enemies of Persia.

Thus Rustam found Rakush. Rustam cared for Rakush as he would have a brother. Rakush carried Rustam into many battles, and was his companion in many great deeds of valour.

The story of Rustam's life, his many adventures and the battles he fought, are all still told and read in Persia.

Sohrab the Smiling One

Of all the adventures that befell Rustam the great hero, perhaps one is worth telling here—that of his love for Princess Tahminah, and of the son that was born to them as a consequence of that love.

Once, tired after a long day's riding and hunting,

Rustam made camp in the wilderness of Turan in the land of the Turks, close to the city of Samengan. Rustam was alone, except for his faithful and devoted horse Rakush. That night, as Rustam slept, and Rakush cropped the pasture near him, there rode by seven knights. They saw a man, fast asleep, and close by him the most magnificent horse ever. Now these seven knights did not realize that it was Rustam they saw asleep, or that it was Rakush grazing at the grass close by. Perhaps if they had known they would not have done what they did next—which was to throw their snares around Rakush's neck and drag him, fighting and kicking, into the city of Samengan and then hiding him. Rakush could have overcome one man, and even two or three, but seven were too many for even this horse to fight.

Next morning, when Rustam awoke, he saw that Rakush had vanished. He looked around and saw the traces of the struggle and realized that Rakush had been stolen. Angry, worried and sad, Rustam followed the tracks left by Rakush and the seven knights, and by and by he found himself at the gates of the city of Samengan.

When the people and the king of Samengan saw Rustam, they recognized him at once, and came out in a procession to welcome him and lead him into their city with honour. But Rustam cried out in anger that he would kill each and every one of them unless they returned Rakush, whom he now knew they hid within their walls. The king reassured Rustam that neither he nor his people had stolen Rakush, but instead, would do all they could to find his horse. He welcomed Rustam with gentle words, and asked him to stay with him in the royal palace while his people searched for Rakush.

Rustam's anger cooled, and he followed the king to the palace, where he was treated like an honoured guest. That night, as Rustam lay fast asleep in the large and comfortable room that he had been given, he was woken by a strange sensation. It seemed to him that the room was full of a strange and heady perfume. Rustam opened his eyes and saw, standing beside his bed was a woman more beautiful than the moon. The room was bathed in the soft light of the lamp that she was carrying. 'Who are you?' asked Rustam in wonder. 'You must be a Peri, for no mortal woman can be so fair!'

At this the woman smiled and said, 'Oh, Rustam, I am no Peri, but Princess Tahminah, daughter of the king of Samengan. Long have I heard of your deeds, and long have I loved you from afar. Now that you have come, you must acknowledge my love, and ask my father for my hand in marriage.'

The very next morning, Rustam asked his host, the king of Samengan, for his daughter's hand in marriage. The king was overjoyed, and very soon Rustam and Princess Tahminah were married.

Upon their wedding night, when they were alone, Rustam gave to Tahminah the onyx that he wore on his arm, and that was known to all the world as his. 'Keep this jewel carefully,' Rustam told the princess. 'If you bear me a daughter, fasten this in her hair and she will always be safe from evil. If you have a son, let him wear it on his arm like his father, and he will be as strong as Saum and as wise as Zal.'

Rustam and Tahminah spent many happy weeks together. Then one day, the king of Samengan sent word that Rakush had been found and was on his way to Rustam. Rustam knew his time for departure had come. He could stay no longer but must ride forth again into the world. Bidding farewell to Tahminah and reminding her about the jewel once more, Rustam saddled Rakush and rode off into the service of the Shah again. To no one did he mention his wedding with Princess Tahminah.

Nine months later, there was born to Tahminah a beautiful little boy who looked exactly like Rustam, his father. The baby was always smiling, so he was called Sohrab. Sohrab grew rapidly and was strong and handsome, just like his father. By the time he was five years old, Sohrab had learnt the use of every weapon and was skilled in the art of battle. And by the time he was ten years old, there was no one who could beat him in games of skill or strength.

Then one day Sohrab came to his mother. He was angry and troubled and said to her, 'I am tall and strong and better than anyone else in all the skills of war. Yet you have not told me who my father is, and what is my lineage. Why have you hidden it all these years?' And Sohrab demanded to know at once his father's name, and the other men from whom he was descended.

Tahminah smiled when she saw Sohrab so angry. He reminded her of his father, Rustam. 'Do not let anger take over your spirit, my son,' said Tahminah. 'You are the son of Rustam, and descended from Saum the Mighty and Zal the White-Haired. In all the world there is no man to equal your father.'

Then Tahminah showed him a letter that Rustam had written to her, and the gold and jewels that he had sent at his birth. And then she said to him, 'My son, cherish these gifts of your father, but let no one know that you are his son. The wicked Afrasiyab, who is Rustam's greatest enemy, now rules Turan and Samengan, our home. Afrasiyab covets also the crown of Persia. He would kill you if he knew who your father is. And if Rustam heard that you were grown so tall and strong, he himself may take you away with him. Either way, I would lose you—and my heart could not bear that. And these are the reasons I have remained silent all these years.'

But Sohrab said, 'You cannot hide the truth forever. I will raise an army of loyal men, and go out in search of my father. I will ride to his aid, and together we will crush the wicked Afrasiyab and deliver Turan and Samengan. Rustam is the noblest man in all the land, and it is right that he wear the crown of Persia. I will help him be crowned king of Persia, and you his queen.'

When Tahminah heard her ten-year-old son speak in this way, she smiled through her tears, and gave him her blessing to go in search of his father.

'I will need a horse to carry me,' said Sohrab, just as his father had done. Tahminah ordered the herds of horses to be led before her son so that he may choose his own. Sohrab tested the horses just as his father had done, by placing his hand upon their backs. But he could not find a single horse that could resist his strength. At last there was brought to him a colt who, said its keeper, was the son of Rakush, Rustam's horse. Sohrab tested the animal, and found that it was strong. He saddled it and leapt upon its back, crying, 'Now that I have a horse like yours, my father, the world will soon be a dangerous place for our enemies!'

Then Sohrab went before his grandfather, the wise and kindly king of Samengan, Tahminah's father, and told him what he intended to do. The king gave his permission and his blessing, and put at Sohrab's disposal all the riches of Samengan.

But the wicked Afrasiyab, under whose yoke groaned Turan and Samengan, and who aspired for the crown of Persia, also heard of Sohrab's plan. He knew that if Sohrab ever came together with Rustam, the two would be invincible. So, calling together all the sly and evil men in his pay, he hatched a plot to make sure that Sohrab would never unite with Rustam. 'Make sure that Sohrab does not recognize his father, and Rustam his son,' commanded Afrasiyab.

Sohrab, unaware that Afrasiyab knew who he was and was planning to trick him, marched out at the head of a small, strong and loyal army to search for Rustam and then combine with him.

Sohrab had many adventures along the way, and with each one, his fame grew, so that people began to say that another hero had arisen, this time from among the Turks.

But Sohrab, for all his valour, was still a boy, and unused to the guile and trickery of older men. Afrasiyab and his agents managed to trick him at every turn, with the result that one day Sohrab found himself facing the army of Rustam, not as a friend but as a foe. And Sohrab did not know that the man whose army he challenged was none other than Rustam his father.

Rustam wondered at the young hero who defied him. He too had heard the tales of his deeds. It was said that the mighty Sohrab looked as though he came from the line of Saum and Zal, though he came out of Turan at the head of an army of Turks. 'Who is this Sohrab?' wondered Rustam. 'Could it be my son, the child of Princess Tahminah of Samengan?' But then he dismissed this thought from his mind. 'My son would be but an infant, barely ten years old,' said Rustam. 'It could not be him at the head of an army! He is still too young!' So Rustam prepared for battle against the Turks of Turan, little knowing his son Sohrab led them.

Thus it happened that Rustam and Sohrab faced each other in single combat, each unaware of who the other was, yet both uneasy in their minds.

Then Rustam said, 'O young man, you are strong and brave and I would not like to kill you. Leave the Turks of Turan and join me, or otherwise you will die at my hands.'

When Rustam spoke to him, Sohrab's heart went out

to him and he asked, 'Tell me who you are. Are you Rustam, son of Zal, descended from Saum the Mighty?'

Rustam, thinking that his reputation might frighten the boy, and wishing to spare him, pretended to be someone else. 'Rustam is a great hero,' he said. 'I am nothing, merely a slave.'

Sohrab bent his head in disappointment. He had been convinced that this mighty warrior before him was Rustam, but the man said he was but a slave!

Then Sohrab and Rustam made ready for combat. They fought long and hard, till all their weapons lay shattered around them. They were evenly matched, and as night fell, neither was the winner. So they agreed to meet again the following day.

Both father and son spent the night racked with doubt.

'Was that not Rustam, my father?' wondered Sohrab. But Afrasiyab's agents convinced Sohrab he was mistaken—that the man he fought was not the great hero Rustam but an unknown king from the border.

'Could that have been my son Sohrab?' wondered Rustam. But remembering that his son was but a child, Rustam let it go.

The following day, and then the day after that, the two heroes fought each other in single combat. The heart of Sohrab was full of doubt—and again and again he sought to find out the true identity of his opponent. But fate and Afrasiyab's wicked schemes kept the truth from him.

At last Rustam won the upper hand. Sohrab lay hurt and

bleeding on the ground, and he knew his last hour had come. As Rustam drew his sword for the final blow, Sohrab sighed and spoke, 'All this fighting is my fault. I had no desire for glory, yet I let myself be tricked into this pointless battle. I had set out to find my father, and now I will never see him. But no matter who you are and where you go, whether you turn yourself into a star and hide in the sky, or become a fish and hide in the sea, my father will find you and kill you. For he is no other than the great hero Rustam, son of Zal the White-Haired and grandson of Saum the Mighty.'

When Rustam heard these words, the sword fell from his hand. He groaned aloud in his anguish, and fell down lifeless beside his son. But soon he came to again and said to Sohrab, 'Do you carry with you a token showing that you are indeed the son of Rustam? For I am Rustam, the father you say you seek.'

Sohrab cried aloud in his misery. 'If you are indeed Rustam, you have killed your own son! And you did it out of your strange reluctance to tell me who you are! Every time I asked you whether you were Rustam, you denied it, and now it is too late. But to see your token, open my armour and upon my arm you will see the onyx you left with Tahminah, my mother.'

Rustam did as Sohrab said, and when he saw the jewel upon the boy's arm, he wept. 'Do not weep,' said Sohrab. 'There is no point in grief any more. It is too late to mend matters.'

Rustam stayed by the side of his dying son till night fell.

Then the men in his camp wondered why he had not returned. 'If he has been killed by this Sohrab, we will destroy the Turks,' they cried. And Rustam's men set out to see what had become of their hero.

Sohrab, when he heard Rustam's men approaching cried out to Rustam for one last favour. 'Do not let your men or the Shah of Persia punish my men of Turan. They came not in enmity to the Shah, but followed me in my search for you, my father. I am dying, and I cannot protect them. So you must promise that you will not let any harm come to them.'

Rustam promised, and rising, went to meet his men. He told them what had happened, and how by mistake he had killed his own son. The men grieved with him and shared his pain. Then Rustam sent a messenger to the men of Turan, and asked them to return peacefully to their homes. But he realized the treachery of Afrasiyab, and how he had tricked his son to fight against him.

Rustam stayed by Sohrab in all the long hours of his agony. And at last, when Sohrab died, Rustam was inconsolable. He laid Sohrab on a bier and carried him home to Zal his father.

Zal saw the army returning, their heads bowed in sorrow, and carrying a bier. Zal knew the mourning was not for his son, for he could see Rustam with the bier, his clothes torn, his head covered with ashes in his grief. Then Rustam told Zal all that had happened, and how he had killed his own son, who was but a child in years though a hero in battle.

Zal and Rustam built for Sohrab a magnificent tomb in the shape of a horse's hoof, and laid him within it, covered in rich brocades. The house of Zal became a house of mourning, and it was a long, long time before Rustam could hold his head high again.

The Education of Princes

This story is taken from the Mahabharata, one of the great Indian epics. It tells of the great war fought between the five Pandav brothers and their hundred cousins, the Kauravas.

Many, many years ago, King Pandu ruled Hastinapura, a small kingdom in what is now northern India. King Pandu was a good and wise king. Under his rule,

Hastinapura prospered and grew rich and powerful. But King Pandu was not a very strong man. For the sake of his health, he retired to the forest with his two queens, Kunti and Madri. He left his kingdom in charge of his brother, the blind Dhritarashtra.

While in the forest, Pandu's queens bore him five sons. These princes were known as the Pandavas, or the sons of Pandu.

Kunti was the mother of the three older sons—Yudhisthira, Bhima and Arjuna. Madri was the mother of the two youngest Pandavas, the twins Nakula and Sahadeva.

Soon after, while the princes were still small children, King Pandu died. Madri, the younger queen, left her two little sons in Kunti's care, and ended her life by throwing herself into the flames of Pandu's funeral pyre.

Kunti was left all alone, without Pandu and without Madri, with five little boys to bring up and look after.

Kunti returned to Hastinapura with the children. Dhritarashtra had now become king after his brother's death. He and his queen, Gandhari, welcomed Kunti and the children warmly and lovingly into the royal household.

Bhishma, the children's great uncle and head of the royal family, welcomed the Pandavas as though they were his own sons. So did Vidura, the children's uncle, half-brother to Pandu and Dhritarashtra.

Dhritarashtra and Gandhari had a hundred sons, known as the Kauravas, and one daughter Duhsala.

The five Pandavas and the hundred Kaurava princes grew up together in the royal palace at Hastinapura. Duryodhana, the oldest of the Kauravas, hated the Pandava princes. He would plot and scheme against them, and Kunti would worry constantly about the safety of her children. But Bhishma, wise and just, ensured the well-being of the Pandava princes.

One day, the Kauravas and the Pandavas were playing ball outside the city walls of Hastinapura. An old well stood just where they were playing. During their game, their ball, as well as Yudhisthira's ring, fell into the well.

'Now what shall we do?' said the princes in annoyance. They gathered round the well and peered in, trying to think of ways and means to get the ball out.

'What's the matter?' asked a voice. The princes looked up to see a short, dark man looking at them. He was a Brahmin, they could tell, because of the sacred thread he wore. But they had never seen him before. He was a complete stranger to all of them.

'We've lost our ball,' explained Yudhisthira. 'And we don't know how to get it out.'

The Brahmin smiled. 'Why, that should be no problem for princes like you,' he said laughing. 'Anyone as skilled in arms as the princes of Hastinapura should know how to take a mere ball out of a well!'

'What does skill in arms have to do with it?' asked the princes.

'Everything!' said the Brahmin. 'Give me an arrow, and I will show you.'

But the princes had no arrows with them that day.

'Never mind,' said the Brahmin. He pointed to a nearby field and said, 'Pick some strong, straight blades of khusha grass growing in that field. The grass will do as well.'

By now the princes were completely mystified and very curious to see what the Brahmin would do. They ran to pick the blades of grass for the dark stranger.

The Brahmin chose the longest and strongest of the blades, and uttering a prayer over it, shot it into the well like an arrow. The blade of grass went straight at the ball and struck it with such force and at such an angle that it flew out of the water, bounced against the wall of the well and jumped straight into the Brahmin's hand.

The princes were amazed. They had never seen anything like it before.

'My ring has also fallen into the well. You can see it shining at the bottom there,' said Yudhisthira, pointing to the bottom of the well. 'Can you get that out as well?'

'Nothing could be easier,' said the stranger.

He again took up a blade of grass, and cut a notch into it. Then, once again saying a prayer over the blade of grass, the unknown Brahmin shot it into the well. The blade of grass hit the ring so that the ring stuck firmly in the notch. The Brahmin then shot several more blades of grass into the well so that they stuck one into the other, forming a long chain. When the chain was long enough, the Brahmin took hold of it and drew the ring out of the well.

Once again, the princes were astonished. 'You are a great archer,' they cried. 'What is your name?'

But the stranger smiled and refused to tell them his name.

'Go,' he said. 'Go and tell the great Bhishma what you have seen here today.'

The princes ran to tell Bhishma all that had happened.

Bhishma realized that this strange Brahmin could be no other than Drona, the son of Bharadwaja, and the greatest archer of all. It was said that Drona had learnt archery from the gods themselves.

Bhishma hurried down to the city gates and welcomed Drona into Hastinapura. He felt Drona was the best person to teach the princes the use of arms. He appointed Drona teacher to the princes. Henceforth, Drona was known as Dronacharya, or 'great teacher'.

A True Archer

One day, Dronacharya gathered his royal pupils around him for a lesson in archery.

He pointed to a bird sitting on a tree in the garden, and said, 'I want you to shoot that bird through the eye.'

He asked Yudhisthira, the eldest prince, to try first. Yudhisthira stepped forward and drew his bow.

'Wait,' commanded Drona. 'First tell me, what do you see?'

'I see the bird, and the branch it is sitting on, the tree

and all its leaves. I see the sky, the earth, my brothers, and you, my teacher,' answered Yudhisthira.

'Put down your bow,' said Dronacharya to Yudhisthira. 'You have much to learn still.'

Next came Duryodhana, the second oldest of the princes. 'What do you see?' asked Drona.

'I see the bird, the tree, the sky, the earth, and my brothers,' answered Duryodhana.

Dronacharya asked him to stand aside as well.

Next, he called Bhima. Bhima's answer was similar to those given by the two older princes, and he too was asked to move aside.

Then came Arjuna's turn.

'What do you see, Arjuna?' asked Dronacharya.

'I see the bird,' said Arjuna.

'What else do you see?' asked Dronacharya.

'Nothing else. I see only the bird,' said Arjuna.

'Do you not see the tree and the sky and the earth?' asked Dronacharya. 'Do you not see me, your teacher? Do you not see your brothers?'

'No,' said Arjuna. 'I see only the bird.'

'What part of the bird do you see, Arjuna?' asked Dronacharya.

'Only the eye,' said Arjuna.

'Well done!' exclaimed Dronacharya. 'You have proved yourself a true archer, Arjuna. For if your eye sees only the target and nothing else around it, your arrow is sure to find its mark!'

Arjuna became Dronacharya's favourite pupil. He grew up to be one of the greatest archers of his age.

Eklavya

At the time that the Pandava princes were growing up in Hastinapura, a young boy called Eklavya lived in the distant forests of what is now southern India.

Eklavya's father was king of the Nishadas, a mountain people who lived in the forests that covered the Vindhya mountains in those days. The Nishadas made their living through hunting and fishing and gathering food in the forest.

Eklavya would often go hunting in the forest with his father and the other men of the tribe. He was very skilled with his weapons, especially with the bow and arrow. But he was not content. He wanted to learn the art of warfare as a true warrior would, but there was no one among the Nishadas who could teach him.

One day, Eklavya heard about the princes of Hastinapura, and their great teacher Drona. It was said that there was no teacher more skilled or more able than he. Eklavya decided to go to Drona and ask him to become his teacher as well.

Eklavya left his home in the mountain forests, and after a long and weary journey north, reached the city of Hastinapura. He found his way to the royal palace. There, in the royal gardens, he saw a short, dark man teaching the use of weapons to the Pandavas and the Kauravas.

Eklavya hid himself behind a bush and watched. The

princes were very able, but more than their skill, it was their teacher who caught Eklavya's attention. He realized that this must be the great Dronacharya himself.

Eklavya came out from behind the bush, and went up to Dronacharya and greeted him with respect. Drona stopped his lesson and politely returning Eklavya's greeting, asked him what he wanted.

Eklavya told him his story—how he would hunt with his father in the forest, how he wanted to learn the use of arms from the greatest teacher on earth, how he had heard of Dronacharya, and travelled hundreds of weary miles to reach him. Drona was very pleased with the boy's desire to learn. 'It will be a pleasure to teach him,' thought Drona to himself.

He smiled at Eklavya. 'What is your name, my son?' he asked. 'Who is your father? Where do you come from?'

'I am Eklavya, sir,' answered the boy. 'My father is king of the Nishadas. We are a mountain tribe and we live far south in the forests that cover the Vindhyas.'

'What! A child of the Nishadas!' cried Drona in horror. 'I cannot teach you, go away at once!'

Eklavya, confused and shaken by Drona's outburst, could only stare at him.

Drona drew himself up haughtily. 'Did you not know,' he asked, 'that I teach only those boys who belong to the warrior caste? The royal princes of Hastinapura are Kshatriyas, proud and noble warriors each, and worthy of my attention. Go away—I will not teach you!'

Slowly, Eklavya walked away from Drona. Hurt and disappointed, he returned to the forests he had come from.

But Eklavya could not stop thinking of Dronacharya and the lesson he had seen him giving the princes in Hastinapura. More than ever, Eklavya became convinced that Drona was the greatest teacher in the world, and the one from whom he must learn the art of archery.

So Eklavya took a lump of clay and made from it an image of Drona. He set the image up in the middle of the forest, and treated it with all the respect and reverence he felt for the real Drona. Eklavya then taught himself archery and the use of weapons. He studied and practised in front of the clay image every day, just as he would have done had the real Drona been his teacher. Many years passed, and Eklavya, all alone in the forest, mastered all the skills of warfare that the royal princes were being taught by Drona in Hastinapura.

One day, Drona took the Pandavas and the Kauravas to the forest to practice hunting. As it happened, this was the same forest in which Eklavya lived, and where he had set up his shrine to Drona. But Drona did not know this. In fact, he had forgotten all about the little boy who had walked so far to learn from him, and whom he had turned away for not being a Kshatriya, so many years ago.

As Drona led the princes through the forest, he noticed arrows stuck in several trees. 'It is almost as though someone has been practising archery here,' thought Drona to himself. He led the princes deeper into the forest, curious to see the person who had shot the arrows. Suddenly, one of Drona's hunting dogs began to bark. Flying out of the air came seven silver arrows that filled the dog's mouth and stopped its barking, yet did not hurt the dog. Drona stopped in wonder. 'Who are you who shoots so well?' called Drona. 'Come, show yourself. We come in peace.'

Out of the bushes stepped Eklavya. He had grown into a tall and athletic young man. Drona did not recognize him.

'Who is your teacher, young man?' asked Drona. 'I would like to meet him. He has taught you well.'

Eklavya bowed low before Drona and invited him to follow him to his forest shrine.

Eklavya led Drona to the clay image he had made. 'This is my teacher,' he said, 'the great Dronacharya himself.'

Drona was astounded to see his own likeness. He turned to look at the young man, who bowed low and touched his feet in reverence. 'I am Eklavya,' he said. 'You turned me away because I was not a Kshatriya, but I have kept your image before me, and learnt my art here in the forest.'

Drona was flattered by Eklavya's devotion, but also unhappy at the young man's skill. He did not like the thought that Eklavya might be better or even as good as the royal princes Drona was teaching.

Drona pretended to be overjoyed at Eklavya's prowess. 'Now that I am here in person, let me test your skill,' he said to Eklavya.

Drona then asked Eklavya to compete against the

princes. Yudhisthira, Bhima, Duryodhana, Duhsasana, all came up and tested their skill against Eklavya's. But Eklavya beat them all. Finally, it was Arjuna's turn. Arjuna was Drona's favourite, and the prince most skilled in archery. But Eklavya beat him as easily as he had beaten the rest.

Arjuna's defeat was unacceptable to Drona. Arjuna had to be the best, by whatever means. Drona determined to disable Eklavya once and for all.

'You have learnt well under your teacher,' he said to Eklavya, pretending to praise him. 'Will you now give your teacher his guru dakshina, his gift to demand by right in return for the learning that he has given you?'

Eklavya knelt before him. 'Ask, and it is yours, my teacher,' he said.

'Give me, then, your right thumb,' said Drona.

Eklavya looked at him. He understood Drona's plan. By demanding Eklavya's right thumb, Drona was making sure that Eklavya could never again lift a bow and arrow to shoot straight and true. Once again, Arjuna would be the best archer of them all, and Eklavya a mere tribal without the right to know the Kshatriya art of warfare.

Eklavya took out his knife, and, without flinching, cut off his right thumb. He handed it without another word to Drona, the great teacher.

Drona and the princes returned to Hastinapura, secure in the knowledge that a potential rival to Arjuna was gone forever. Eklavya returned to his people in the forest.

This happened many thousands of years ago. We still remember Eklavya for his dedication to learning and his devotion to the person he had acknowledged as his teacher.

But what of Drona? Was he really a great teacher?

Siddhartha and the Swan

Gautam Buddha, the founder of Buddhism, was born in 563 BC in the kingdom of Kapilavastu, in what is now Nepal. There are many stories about Buddha and his followers.

More than two thousand and five hundred years ago, the Sakya king Sudhodhana ruled over the kingdom of Kapilavastu. King Sudhodhana and his queen, Maya, had no children.

One night, as Queen Maya lay sleeping, she had a strange dream. She dreamt that a beautiful baby elephant, as white as snow, came down from the sky and entered her body. At once, music began to play, trees and bushes blossomed with flowers, and lotuses covered the lakes. The whole world began to celebrate.

The next morning, the queen described her strange dream. The Brahmin priests foretold that soon a son would be born to her, a son who would become either a great king or a great sage. A few months later, the queen gave birth to a beautiful baby boy. King Sudhodhana and Queen Maya named their son Siddhartha.

The king and queen surrounded their son with every luxury and comfort that they could think of. Siddhartha's days were spent in the palace and its beautiful gardens, playing and learning with his cousins, friends and companions. His best friends were his cousin Ananda, his squire Chandak and his horse Kantak.

Siddhartha was a kind and gentle child, and everyone who met him loved him, except his cousin Devadatta. Devadatta hated Siddhartha. He hated his kindness and his compassion, and the fact that he was loved so dearly by everyone in the palace. Devadatta used every opportunity he could get to pick a fight with Siddhartha, or to create trouble for him.

One lovely spring morning, Siddhartha was playing by the river that flowed through the palace gardens. He saw a group of swans floating gracefully on the river.

Siddhartha stopped to watch them. The great white birds swam slowly down the river, their feathers edged with gold in the bright sunshine. 'Oh, you're beautiful,' whispered Siddhartha to the swans. Siddhartha sat down by the riverbank to watch the birds.

Suddenly an arrow came whizzing out of the air, and pierced the biggest, most beautiful of the swans. Siddhartha cried out, and ran into the river towards the bird. The poor swan was thrashing his wings in fear and pain. It couldn't swim, it couldn't fly—the arrow had broken one of its wings.

Siddhartha held his hands out to the injured bird, calling softly to calm it down. He held the bird tenderly in his arms and waded out to the riverbank. He quieted the swan, and then gently pulled the arrow out of its wing. Using a stick for a splint, and a strip torn from his clothing for a bandage, Siddhartha set and bound the wing of the swan.

Meanwhile, Devadatta came running up in search of his arrow. He too had seen the swans from a distance, and had decided to practise his shooting skills on the beautiful birds.

'That swan belongs to me,' said Devadatta. 'I shot it, not you.'

'No,' said Siddhartha. 'It belongs to me. I saved it.'

'Very well,' said Devadatta. 'Let us go to our guru. He will tell you that the swan is mine because it is my arrow that hit it!'

The two children took the injured swan to their guru.

The guru heard Devadatta's tale and turned to Siddhartha.

'Well, Siddhartha,' asked the teacher. 'What do you have to say?'

'Devadatta hurt the swan,' said Siddhartha. 'The swan was doing him no harm! It was swimming on the river, looking so beautiful. Why did Devadatta shoot it? I will not let him have it, he will hurt it again. I have made it well—so now it is mine.'

The teacher smiled when he heard what Siddhartha had to say.

'The swan belongs to Siddhartha,' he said. 'Siddhartha has saved its life, and cared for it and made it well. Devadatta has hurt it, and sought to destroy it. Nobody can own a living being, except the one who loves it. So the swan remains with Siddhartha.'

Devadatta was furious. He stomped off, swearing he would get even with Siddhartha one day.

But Siddhartha only smiled. He had saved the swan. He looked after the bird till its broken wing was mended, and then released it back into the river.

Siddhartha grew up to fulfil the prophecy of his birth—he became a great sage, among the greatest of them all. Siddhartha became Gautama Buddha.

Horus and the Throne of Egypt

Egyptian mythology has been pieced together by scholars through inscriptions on the walls of pyramids, on coffin lids and on papyrus scrolls. The story of Horus may be found in bits and pieces all over Egypt, with slight variations. Plutarch, the Greek writer who lived from AD 40 to AD 120, has also retold the story of Horus, combining the original Egyptian tale with Greek ideas and concepts.

Osiris, eldest son of Geb the Earth and Nut the Sky, ruled the land of Egypt, and took for his queen his sister Isis.

Together, Osiris and Isis put an end to war and strife, and brought peace and plenty to Egypt. Osiris taught his people how to make wine and bread. He built towns and cities, temples and gardens, and laid down just laws for his people to live by. Isis taught the women how to grind corn and spin flax and weave cloth, and the men to cure disease. Under the rule of Osiris and Isis, all Egypt flourished.

Till one day came Seth, younger son of Geb and Nut, brother to Osiris and Isis. Seth saw the land of Egypt prosper, and wanted it for himself. Seth was strong and cruel and ruthless. He turned himself into a fearsome creature, with four legs, and a scorpion's sting. As Osiris strolled by the river at Nedyet, Seth attacked and killed him. Seth then hid his brother's body, and claimed for himself the throne of Egypt. He took as his queen his sister Nephthys, Isis's twin.

But Nephthys could not rejoice with Seth. She had loved her brother Osiris, and did not think Seth had done right to murder him. She joined Isis in her grief, and together the sisters mourned the death of Osiris.

Isis, heartbroken, angry and vengeful, determined to find the body of Osiris, and bring him back to life. She swore she would have a son who would avenge his father's murder, and claim the throne of Egypt as his rightful inheritance.

Isis and Nephthys roamed the land of Egypt, searching for the body of Osiris, till finally they found it at Abydos.

Then, turning herself into a kite, Isis created the breath of life with her wings, and brought Osiris back to life. Osiris woke up, and tenderly embraced his queen. From their embrace was conceived a child, their son Horus, within Isis. Osiris's time on earth was over—Egypt now belonged to his son. So Osiris descended into Duat, the underworld, there to rule as king of the underworld for all eternity.

Isis dreamt that she would give birth to a hawk, who would soar up, up into the sky, far above the land of Egypt. His eyes would be the sun and the moon, and with him would be identified the throne of Egypt forever. She called her son Horus, which means 'Far-Above-One'.

The Seven Scorpions and More

One day, Isis was busy weaving the linen wrappings for Osiris's body, with her little baby beside her. Thoth, the god of wisdom, saw her from his place in the sun's boat in the sky. Down came Thoth to Isis and said, 'Do not show your little son to the world! Hide him, hide yourself—keep yourself safe from Seth, who has not forgotten and who will stop at nothing to keep the throne of Egypt. Give your son a fair chance to grow into a man, so that he may then avenge his father, and rightfully claim for himself the throne of Egypt!'

Isis listened to Thoth. She left her home that very evening, with the baby Horus, and an escort of seven scorpions to protect her.

'We must be very careful,' said Isis to the scorpions. 'Seth must not hear of our whereabouts, for if he finds the baby, he will kill him. Make sure you do not speak to any strangers on the way, for on no account must we let our presence be known!'

The scorpions nodded their understanding and prepared to escort Isis and Horus safely into hiding. Three of the scorpions, Petet, Tjetet and Matet, walked in front of Isis and the baby to make sure her path was safe. Two others, Mesetet and Mesetef, walked under her palanquin, while the remaining two, Tefen and Befen, brought up the rear.

Finally, Isis, her son, and the escort of scorpions reached a place called the Town of the Two Sisters, on the Nile delta. Night was falling and Isis was in need of shelter. A large house stood in the middle of the town. It belonged to a rich noblewoman. Isis wondered if the rich woman would put her up for the night, but the rich woman refused, and banged her door shut.

A poor peasant woman had also seen Isis arrive. When she saw that Isis had no place to stay that night, she ran to her and asked her to stay with her. Isis accepted the poor woman's offer and took shelter in her hut along with her son and her loyal escort of seven scorpions.

The seven scorpions adored Isis. They were furious with the rich woman and her rudeness in refusing Isis shelter and decided to take revenge. That night, when the town slept, the scorpions woke up. Six of them loaded their poison onto the sting of the seventh, Tefen. Silently, quietly,

Tefen crawled under the door of the rich woman's house. He crept across the floor and into the room where the rich woman slept with her little son. Tefen crawled up the bedclothes, and stung the rich woman's son, unloading the poison of all the seven scorpions into his body.

The child screamed in pain, and the rich woman awoke with a start. She saw the scorpion escaping through the door and realized that her child had been stung. Now, a scorpion's sting can kill, and the rich woman knew that. She wept and cried and she ran through the town, knocking on every door, begging for help. 'Save my child,' she cried. 'Oh please, someone help! Help my child! Don't let him die!' But no one answered her cries for help.

No one, that is, except Isis.

Isis understood at once what had happened—that the rich woman was being punished by her scorpions. 'But why should a child suffer for his mother's foolishness?' said Isis to herself. 'It is not the child's fault that the mother is rude and arrogant!' Isis hurried to the rich woman's house and took the crying child into her lap. Holding him close, she uttered words of magic over him, till the poison left him, and he was well again. The rich woman begged forgiveness, and in gratitude and contrition offered all her wealth to Isis and the peasant girl who had given Isis shelter.

In ancient Egypt, people would use Isis's spell to cure their children of scorpion stings, in the hope that they could make them well just as Isis had made the rich woman's son well.

But the spell did not always work, even for Isis. One day, she hid her little son in the papyrus marshes of Khemmis in the Nile delta, and went to search for food. She came back a while later to find that Horus had been stung to death by scorpions. Isis screamed in grief and terror. Her screams were so loud that they were heard by Re the sun god, as he rode in his boat across the sky. Out of concern for Isis, Re stopped his boat, and the earth was plunged into darkness.

Thoth, god of wisdom, and ever Isis's friend, left Re's boat and came down to help her. He uttered powerful spells over Horus, and threatened that the earth would stay dark forever unless Horus came back to life. At this threat of Thoth's, the poison retreated from Horus's body, and the child awoke. Thoth charged the people of Khemmis with Horus's care. 'Look after him with more than your lives,' he said, 'for Horus holds within him the destiny of the world.' So saying, Thoth returned to Re's boat, which once again set off across the sky, bringing back light and warmth to the earth.

How Horus Won the Throne

All through Horus's childhood, Isis kept him safe from harm—from snakes and scorpions and crocodiles, and from Seth's schemes and plans. Till one day she felt that Horus was old enough to challenge his uncle and claim for himself the throne of Egypt.

Horus presented his claim to a divine tribunal presided over by the sun god Re. Thoth, the god of wisdom, and Shu the god of air, both declared Horus to be the rightful king of Egypt. Isis couldn't believe her ears—that at long last Horus was getting that which was rightfully his. She prepared the north wind to take the good news to her husband Osiris, king of the underworld. But Re stopped her, saying he hadn't yet made up his mind.

'Horus, as Osiris's son, is the rightful king of Egypt!' protested Thoth. 'Osiris was king, and it is only right that his son be king after him!'

'Ah, but Seth is stronger!' said Re. 'He is also older, and therefore wiser than Horus, who is still little more than a child! Seth will make a better king.' Re's favourite was obviously Seth.

The gods argued back and forth for eighty years. They could not decide one way or the other—Thoth and Shu believed Horus to be the rightful king, while Re felt Seth had a better claim to the throne because of his age and his strength. Unable to decide, the tribunal of gods wrote a letter to the goddess Neith asking her to decide between Horus and Seth.

'The throne of Egypt must be restored to Horus, son of Osiris, to whom it rightfully belongs,' wrote Neith. 'To Seth—give him treasure, and let him marry the sun god's daughters, Anat and Astarte.' Neith was firmly on Horus's side. 'The sky will fall on Egypt,' she warned in her letter, 'unless the throne be given to Horus.' Still, Re was not convinced.

'The throne is mine by virtue of my strength,' declared Seth. 'Let Horus prove that he is better than I and he can have the throne!' he challenged.

Horus, secure in his belief that the throne was his, and determined to avenge his father, agreed. 'Challenge me to what you will,' he cried to his uncle. 'I will prove you the weaker!'

'I dare you to stay underwater with me for three months,' cried Seth to Horus. 'The one who comes up first for a breath of air shall give up the throne of Egypt!' And Seth turned himself into a gigantic hippopotamus and sank under the waters of the Nile. Horus, accepting the challenge, did the same—he turned himself into a large hippopotamus and taking a deep breath, sank into the Nile.

Isis watched the hippos worriedly. She did not trust Seth at all. So, picking up a copper harpoon, she threw it into the water, intending to wound Seth. Instead, she hit Horus by mistake. Isis realized her mistake and withdrew the harpoon and healed his wound with her magic.

Isis threw the harpoon again, and this time she hit Seth. But Seth was her brother after all, however evil, and Isis could not hurt him. So she withdrew her harpoon once again, and healed Seth's wounds as well.

At this, Horus rose out of the water, angrily demanding to know whose side Isis was on. He was so angry with his mother that he cut off her head—at which she turned into a statue of stone. Now it was Seth's turn to be angry. Furious with Horus for hurting his sister, Seth chased him across the desert, and gouged his eyes out and buried them in the sand. He left Horus to die—blind and helpless, and full of grief for cutting off his mother's head.

But the goddess Hathor found Horus, and rubbing his eyes with gazelle milk, restored his vision and his health. Meanwhile Isis too had been miraculously restored to life.

Seth then suggested that Horus and he make boats of stone. 'The one whose boat sails the farthest shall get the throne of Egypt,' he declared.

Horus agreed. He made a boat of pinewood, and cleverly painted it to look like stone. Seth was amazed to see Horus's boat, apparently made of stone, floating down the Nile. So he cut off a mountain peak and hollowed it out, making a boat that was seventy metres long. But Seth's boat sank. Furious, Seth realized the trick that Horus had played on him, and turning himself into a giant red hippopotamus, smashed Horus's boat. Horus picked up a harpoon, and prepared to launch it, to kill Seth and to end the dispute once and for all. But the gods prevented him.

Tired of this endless bickering, Thoth, the god of wisdom, persuaded the sun god Re to write to Osiris in the underworld, asking him to finally decide between his brother and his son. Osiris commanded that the gods decide in favour of Horus his son. 'Or,' threatened Osiris, 'I will unleash my fearsome servants, thirsty for blood, to pluck out your hearts and bring them to me.' Osiris reminded Re that he was king of the underworld, where all beings, human or divine must ultimately descend, and through which even the stars of the sky and Re himself must every day pass.

Re could not take Osiris's threats lightly, and finally gave his decision in favour of Horus. Seth was bound in chains and led before the gods as Isis's prisoner, where he relinquished the throne of Egypt in favour of his nephew Horus.

Horus became king of Egypt, and ever after, the throne of Egypt was called the Horus throne. Each succeeding king of Egypt was identified with Horus while he ruled, and with his father Osiris, king of the underworld, after he was dead.

As for Seth, Re still favoured him, and took him with him to ride in his sun boat across the sky where his voice became the thunder in the heavens. You can still hear him during a thunderstorm, rumbling and roaring across the sky.

Heracles

Heracles is one of the greatest heroes of Greek mythology. He is credited with deeds of great bravery that no one else, mortal or immortal, had been able to do. His most famous exploits are the Twelve Labours that he performed for his cousin King Eurysthens.

The Romans later took Heracles and his exploits into their own mythology. They called him Hercules.

Alcmene, wife of Amphitryon, gave birth to twin sons, Alcaeus and Iphicles.

Some say that Alcaeus was the older twin, some say he was the younger—but all agree that he was the brighter, livelier, stronger child. This was so because Alcaeus was really the son of Zeus, king of the gods, who had tricked Alcmene into loving him by pretending to be her husband Amphitryon.

Iphicles, however, was the son of Amphitryon, Alcmene's husband.

Now, Hera, queen of the gods and wife of Zeus, was insanely jealous of any other woman her husband might have loved. Alcmene was terrified that Hera, hearing that she had given birth to Zeus's son, would harm her in some way. So one night, as the world lay asleep, Alcmene took her newborn son Alcaeus, and crept out of the palace. She crept out of the city, and there, in the empty fields beyond the city wall, she left her infant son to die.

Zeus, king of the gods, was watching. He had no intention that his son should die. In fact, he had foretold that this child of his would be the greatest hero ever born. So Zeus asked Athena, his favourite daughter, to help him. Athena, who adored her father, agreed to do as he said.

The very next morning, Athena took Hera for a walk, to the very fields where Alcmene had left baby Alcaeus to die. 'Oh, look!' suddenly cried Athena, pretending to be surprised and running towards the baby lying on the ground. 'What a beautiful, healthy baby! Who would have left him to die, I wonder?' She picked the baby up, and gently cradled him in her arms. 'His mother must have been mad, to leave such a lovely child to die!' cried Athena.

Hera came running up, to take a look. 'What a lovely baby,' she exclaimed.

'He must be hungry,' said Athena. 'You have milk. Give the poor baby a feed!'

Hera held out her arms and suckled the hungry child. But Alcaeus sucked at her breast with such force, that Hera cried out in pain. She pulled the child from her, and a spurt of milk flew across the sky becoming the Milky Way. Hera realized, too late, that she had been tricked. This was no ordinary baby, but Zeus's son.

But the child, having drunk the milk of the goddess, had now become immortal, which meant that he would never die.

Athena took the child from Hera with a smile, and returned him to Alcmene. 'Look after your son well,' she said to Alcmene. 'He will be great one day.'

Since the baby Alcaeus had been suckled by the goddess Hera, he was renamed 'Heracles', which means the 'Glory of Hera', in her honour. Therefore, he is also sometimes regarded as her son.

One evening, when the twins Heracles and Iphicles were about eight months old, their mother Alcmene fed them and washed them and sang them to sleep in their father Amphitryon's big bronze shield.

Hera, queen of the gods, hated Alcmene and the baby Heracles. So that night, as the babies slept peacefully in Amphitryon's bronze shield, Hera sent two blue-scaled serpents to kill Heracles.

The serpents slithered to Amphitryon's house. The gates opened as they approached—and the serpents slithered through, into the house and through the rooms, till they found the twins asleep all by themselves in their father's shield. The snakes arched themselves over the babies, their eyes shooting flames, their forked tongues darting in and out, their fangs dripping poison.

Zeus was as always watching over his son Heracles. He flooded the room with light, and the twins awoke. Iphicles, Amphitryon's son, screamed in fright when he saw the monster serpents. But Heracles, Zeus's son, gurgled with delight. He reached out and grabbed the serpents by their necks, and squeezed them and played with them as with a toy, laughing happily.

Meanwhile, Alcmene, hearing Iphicles's cries, ran in—to find Heracles lying in his crib with the serpents clutched in his baby hands. Heracles was gurgling happily, but the monster snakes were dead.

Next morning, Alcmene called Teiresias, a wise old man who could see the future, and told him what had happened. Teiresias then foretold the future greatness of Heracles. As we know, Heracles went on to become one of the greatest heroes ever, ridding the world of evil monsters that had terrified men and gods alike for ages. When he had fulfilled his destiny, his father Zeus took him up on Mt. Olympus, where live the gods of ancient Greece. There, Heracles lives even now.

Flight to the Sun

This is a story from Greek mythology.

Long ago, in ancient Crete, there lived for a while a brilliant and talented man called Daedalus. Daedalus, who had been taught by the goddess Athena herself, was a sculptor, an architect, a scientist and an inventor. It is said that he had even invented robots—statues that could move like real people, and do almost everything that human beings could do.

The king of Crete, Minos, valued Daedalus's skills greatly. Daedalus built for him magnificent palaces and wonderful buildings. At King Minos's request, Daedalus built as well the Labyrinth. This was a wonderful palace full of complex and intricate corridors. It was said that no one, who once entered the Labyrinth, could ever find his way out again. At the heart of this maze, King Minos imprisoned the dreadful monster known as the Minotaur, who was half-man and half-bull. King Minos greatly honoured Daedalus especially for this Labyrinth.

Now, every nine years there came to Crete from Attica a ship carrying seven young men and seven young women. Long ago, the people of Attica had killed King Minos's son. In return, Minos had demanded that seven young men and seven young women be sacrificed to him once every nine years. Minos would throw the young men and women to the Minotaur, who would devour them, bones and all. The people of Attica submitted to this cruel penalty, for there was no one who could stand up to the might of Minos and the horror of the Minotaur. Till one year, Theseus, a brave young man, volunteered to go to Crete and fight the Minotaur.

King Minos threw Theseus and the other young men and women from Attica into the Labyrinth, sure that none would escape. But Minos's daughter, Ariadne, had seen Theseus and fallen in love with him. Ariadne did not want

Theseus to die. She knew that the only man who could help him find his way out of the Labyrinth alive was Daedalus. Daedalus advised Ariadne to give Theseus a ball of string, which he should unwind as he went into the Labyrinth in search of the monster. Ariadne did as Daedalus suggested. Theseus killed the Minotaur, and found his way out of the Labyrinth again with the help of the string he had unwound.

Minos was furious when he heard that Theseus had killed the Minotaur and escaped. To save themselves from Minos's wrath, Theseus and Ariadne fled Crete. But Daedalus could not get away. He was taken prisoner and thrown into the Labyrinth, along with his young son Icarus.

'Oh, father,' wept Icarus. 'How much longer do we have to stay here? I hate this place—it smells!'

Icarus was right—the Labyrinth did smell. It smelt of old bones and feathers and stale meat—leftovers of the Minotaur's huge meals. It smelt of the fear of hundreds of men and women who had been devoured by the beast. And worst of all, it smelt of the Minotaur himself. Even though the creature was dead, killed by Theseus, the entire Labyrinth still smelt of his foul presence.

Daedalus sighed. He knew he could find his way out of the Labyrinth. That would not be difficult for him since he was the one who had designed it, and knew every turn of the long, winding, bewildering maze of corridors that had so effectively imprisoned the Minotaur. The real problem, Daedalus knew, was how to escape from the island of Crete.

King Minos was a powerful and cruel man. Daedalus knew Minos would have every road, every port, every harbour watched for Daedalus and his son. Escape across land or sea was impossible.

'That leaves only the air,' sighed Daedalus to himself in frustration. 'If only we could fly like birds!' Slowly, a thought, an idea began to take shape in this inventor's brain. Suppose, just suppose, he could make himself and Icarus fly? Could they then not escape the cruel Minos?

'Come, Icarus,' cried Daedalus to his son. 'I have an idea—and perhaps a plan that may work!' Daedalus then spent the next few days up on the highest tower of the Labyrinth, looking out at the sky and studying the flight of birds. 'Look how they flap their wings, Icarus,' he would say. 'Look how effortlessly they glide through the air.' Daedalus studied the shape of their wings, and how they bent and curved to let the air flow over them and lift the birds into the sky. Icarus sat with Daedalus, and watched and listened and learnt.

At last, Daedalus had learnt all that he wanted to know about birds and how they fly. 'We're going to fly out of here,' he told his little son. 'We're going to make ourselves some wings, and then fly out of here like birds!'

'So we need feathers!' cried Icarus.

'Yes,' said Daedalus. 'Luckily for us, the Labyrinth is full of them!' The Labyrinth was full of old feathers, of the birds the Minotaur had eaten when he had been alive.

Daedalus and Icarus collected the feathers. They cleaned them and smoothed them and sorted them into piles. Then Daedalus set to work to make the wings. The quill feathers he strung together with thread, but the smaller feathers he stuck together with wax. At last the wings were ready, a large pair for Daedalus, and a smaller pair for Icarus.

Daedalus tied on Icarus's wings, and then his own. He held his son close and hugged him. 'Now, son,' he said, 'be careful as you fly. Don't fly too low or the sea will soak the feathers, and don't fly too high or the sun will melt the wax that holds them together.' Icarus nodded and promised to do as his father said. 'Follow me and do as I do,' said Daedalus, 'and you will be safe.'

Father and son climbed up to the very highest tower of the Labyrinth, and watching for the right moment, launched themselves into the air. The wings were perfect. Daedalus and Icarus glided in the breeze like giant birds. Then, setting course in a north-easterly direction, Daedalus flew far away from Crete, with Icarus close behind.

Daedalus and Icarus flew over land and sea, over forests, fields and farms. Shepherds tending their flock on mountainsides, and farmers working their fields in the valleys looked up and saw them, and thought they were gods, who flew so effortlessly in the sky.

At first, Icarus was very careful to follow his father's advice, and made sure he kept close behind Daedalus and flew neither too low nor too high. He loved the feel of his wings as they carried him through the air, and after a while, as he grew more sure of his wings, he wanted to fly as freely as the birds. He wanted to wheel and dip and hover, and soar high up in the sky.

And very soon, caught up in the joy of flying, Icarus forgot his father's advice. He flew up and up and up into the sky, higher and higher and higher. He loved the power of his wings beating strongly and flawlessly in the wind. 'How far below is the sea,' thought Icarus to himself as he looked down at the world.

Icarus flew still higher. The sun shone brighter and hotter, and hotter and brighter, till Icarus was quite warm. Still he did not remember his father's warning not to fly too high. Alas! Icarus then flew much too close to the sun. The sun's fierce heat melted the wax that held the feathers together, and Icarus's perfect wings fell apart.

Down, down, down he plummeted through the air, into the deep blue sea below.

Meanwhile, Daedalus, flying steadily, realized his son was no longer with him. Frantically, he searched the skies—and saw him, soaring ever higher, a tiny speck close to the sun. Before Daedalus could call out to him to stop, to fly down, he saw Icarus fall, fall, fall, down into the sea.

Daedalus flew down to the waves where Icarus had fallen, and wept. The sea threw up Icarus—but it was too late. Icarus was dead, drowned in the sea. The feathers from his wings floated sadly on the waves.

Daedalus was heartbroken. He gathered up his little son in his arms, and carried him to a nearby island where he buried him.

The island is to this day called Icaria, after Icarus, and the sea into which he fell is known as the Icarian Sea.

Daedalus continued his flight, and successfully managed to escape from Crete and Minos. He lived for many years, and built many magnificent temples and buildings all over the Mediterranean region. Many of his works can still be seen in Sardinia. They are called Daedaleia.

The Sons of Mars

The story of Romulus and Remus is the story of the founding of the city of Rome. According to Plutarch, the Roman biographer, Rome was founded on Palatine Hill on 21 April 753 BCE.

All over Rome, even today, you can see statues, paintings and frescoes of the she-wolf and the two babies.

Many, many hundreds of years ago, in the city of Alba, in what is now southern Italy, there ruled King

Numitor. Numitor was a good king, but he had an evil brother called Amulius.

Amulius wanted the throne of Alba for himself. So one night, while the Numitor slept, Amulius marched into the palace with some soldiers and took the king prisoner.

Amulius also took prisoner the beautiful princess Rhea Silvia, Numitor's daughter. Amulius forced Rhea Silvia to become a Vestal Virgin. The Vestal Virgins were princesses who gave up the world and never married or had children. They spent their whole lives in the service of the goddess Vesta. He was afraid that if Rhea Silvia were to marry and have children, those children would one day take back the throne of Alba from him.

One day, Mars, the god of war, and the avenger of the wronged, heard the sad tale of Numitor and his beautiful daughter Rhea Silvia. He saw Rhea Silvia walking in the gardens of the Vestals's palace, and fell in love with her. That night, as the world lay asleep, Mars came to Rhea Silvia, and from his love, Rhea Silvia conceived twin sons.

When Amulius heard that Rhea Silvia was pregnant, he was furious. 'Bind her in chains and take her away!' he ordered his soldiers. 'Throw her into the darkest prison. Watch her night and day!'

For nine long months, Rhea Silvia lay bound in chains in the deepest, darkest prison in Alba. Till one day her babies were born—two beautiful little boys.

But the wicked Amulius ordered that the boys be killed

at once. 'Throw them into the River Tiber,' he commanded. 'Let the river take them.'

The soldiers, though full of pity for the beautiful princess and her babies, did not dare disobey Amulius. They put the babies into a basket of reeds and set them afloat on the Tiber. Amulius was sure the twins would drown, for the Tiber was a deep and swift-flowing river. He was satisfied he had rid himself of the last threat to his kingship.

But it was the very violence of the river that saved the babies. The force of the water threw the basket up onto the riverbank, at the foot of the Palatine Hill, where it came to rest under a fig tree. There, a she-wolf found the babies.

The she-wolf lay down beside the twins, and suckled them, and kept them warm. A woodpecker stood guard over them in the branches of the fig tree. The wolf and the woodpecker were sacred animals, sent there by Mars himself, to look after his sons and keep them safe.

One day, a shepherd called Faustulus was passing by. He heard the babies gurgling and playing, and went to investigate. There, under the fig tree, lay the babies, being suckled by their foster mother, the she-wolf.

The she-wolf and the woodpecker saw the shepherd and knew that their task was done. The babies had been found and would now be loved and looked after. The she-wolf walked off into the wilderness, never to be seen again. The woodpecker flew away.

Faustulus took the children home to his wife Acca Larentia.

'Look,' he called to his wife. 'Look what I found beside the Tiber today. Two beautiful boys—abandoned!' And he told his wondering wife how he had heard the babies and then found them under the fig tree, being suckled by a she-wolf.

Faustulus and Acca Larentia had no children of their own. So they decided to adopt the twins and bring them up as their own sons. They named the boys Romulus and Remus.

Romulus and Remus grew up with the other shepherd lads. They were tall and handsome, and skilled in sport and hunting. Of the two, Romulus was the more level-headed, Remus the more impetuous.

One day, the brothers and their friends, the shepherd boys, were attacked by a band of robbers. Romulus managed to escape, but Remus was captured and handed over to the wicked king Amulius.

Numitor, the deposed king, and the twins' own grandfather, heard of the capture of Remus, and came to know that Remus was one of twins found abandoned by the river Tiber. Numitor realized at once that Remus must be one of his own grandsons.

Meanwhile, Faustulus the shepherd had also told Romulus the truth about his birth and how he had found the twins by the river and decided to bring them up as his own sons.

Romulus, furious at his brother's capture, attacked Amulius. When the people saw that there was someone brave enough to stand up to the wicked king, they came running to help him. In the battle that followed—between Romulus and the people of Alba on one side, and Amulius and his soldiers on the other—the wicked Amulius was killed.

The people of Alba welcomed back Numitor as their true king, and gave him back the crown of Alba. Numitor embraced Romulus and Remus as his own true grandsons, the sons of his daughter Rhea Silvia and the god Mars.

Thus Romulus and Remus found once again their true place in the world.

The Founding of Rome

When the twins grew to manhood, they went to their grandfather Numitor and said, 'Grandfather, we miss the hills and forests of our childhood. Give us permission to return there, so that we may found a new city in the place where we grew up.'

Numitor gave his grandsons his permission and his blessing, and the twins set out for the hills and forests of their childhood.

Romulus and his friends explored the Palatine Hill, while Remus and his friends explored the Aventine Hill. High in the sky, some vultures appeared. Six of them flew off towards the Aventine where Remus stood, and twelve of them hovered over Romulus on the Palatine.

Romulus took this as a sign from the gods that he was to build the new city on his chosen site. So he yoked a bull and a cow to a plough, and drew a furrow in the ground to mark the boundaries of his new city.

But Remus was jealous that the gods had chosen his brother and not him. He laughed at Romulus and mocked him. 'Your city will never be strong or great or beautiful,' he teased Romulus. 'It will fall into enemy hands as easily as I can jump across the furrow you have drawn to mark its boundaries.' Laughing and taunting, Remus jumped over the sacred furrow that Romulus had drawn. This made Romulus so angry that he picked up his spear and killed Remus on the spot.

Romulus then went on to found his city, and gave it his own name. The city still stands. It is called Rome.

The Legend of the Dwarf

The Maya or Mayan people are the native people of Central America, living in southern Mexico, Guatemala, and northern Belize. As early as 1500 BC, the Mayans had settled into villages and had agriculture and farming. By AD 200, they had built great cities with palaces, temples, courts for playing ball, and pyramids. They cultivated crops, worked gold and copper, and used a hieroglyphic writing which has now been mostly deciphered. Before the Spanish conquest of the Americas in the early sixteenth century, the Mayans possessed one of the greatest civilizations of the western hemisphere.

We know about Maya civilization through the ruins that have been found of their great cities, of the fragments of Mayan writing that has been discovered, and through stories and legends that have been handed down through time or preserved in books such as the *Popol Vuh*.

The Legend of the Dwarf is a story of the Yucatec Mayans, the Mayan people who lived in the Yucatan peninsula of Mexico. The story is set in the ancient Yucatan city of Uxmal, where even today the ruins of a great palace or temple can be seen, which is the Dwarf's House of the story. The old woman is probably the Rain Goddess, the Dwarf the Man of the Sun. In Yucatan, dwarfs were sacred to the Sun, and often sacrificed to him.

Many hundreds of years ago, there lived an old woman, all alone in a tiny hut. She had no children, and no one to ask after her. The old woman would weep night and day for a child, but of course, with no result.

One day, she took an egg, wrapped it carefully in cotton cloth, and put it in a corner of her hut. Night and day the old woman looked after the egg, in the hope that maybe it would give her a child. But nothing happened, and every day the old woman grew more and more unhappy.

One morning, as she went to look at the egg, she found that it had broken—and in its shell sat the tiniest, loveliest baby boy that anyone could imagine. The baby saw the old woman and smiled and held out its tiny arms. The old woman was delighted—here at last was the child she had wanted for so long.

The old woman loved the child dearly, and looked after it so carefully and so well, that by the time it was a year old, it could walk and talk as well as any grown up. But for some strange reason, no one knows what, the baby stopped growing. He remained as tiny as a one-year-old for the rest of his life. He began to be called the 'Dwarf'

The old woman did not care. She still loved the baby devotedly. 'You will be a great king one day, my child,' she told him, sure that the baby was destined for great things.

One day, the old woman said to the Dwarf, 'Go to the king's palace, my son, and challenge him to test his strength against yours.'

The Dwarf protested. 'How can I challenge the king, Mother?' he said horrified. 'He is greater and much stronger than I.'

But the old woman insisted, and the Dwarf was forced to do as she said.

The king smiled at the child's challenge, and asked him to lift a heavy stone. The Dwarf went weeping to the old woman. 'How can I lift that heavy stone?' he asked.

'If the king can lift it, so can you,' said the old woman, and sent him back to the palace.

And sure enough, the Dwarf was able to lift the heavy stone.

The king gave him many more tasks to do, but anything the king could do, the Dwarf could do as well.

When the king saw that this tiny little child could do

whatever he himself could do, he was afraid, and very angry. He decided to get rid of the child by asking him to do something impossible.

'Build me a palace taller and higher and more magnificient than any in my city,' the king commanded the Dwarf. 'You must do this in one night. If the palace is not ready by tomorrow morning, you will die.' The king thought that the Dwarf would never be able to fulfil his command and so would lose his head.

The Dwarf was terribly frightened. He ran home to the old woman and wept. 'How will I ever build a palace that high or that magnificient?' he cried. 'I will surely die tomorrow.'

Bu the old woman comforted the child and said, 'Go to sleep, my son. It will be done by the morning.' The Dwarf did as his mother said and went to sleep.

The next morning, he woke up in a beautiful palace, taller, higher and more magnificent than any in the king's city. This is the palace the ruins of which can still be seen in the city of Uxmal.

When the king looked out of his window that morning, he saw the new palace towering up to the sky. He was amazed. 'I must think of another way to get rid of him,' he thought.

The king then sent for the Dwarf and asked him to collect two bundles of cogoiol, a sort of hardwood. 'With one bundle I shall strike you on the head,' said the king to the Dwarf. 'And if you survive, you may strike me on the head with the other.'

The Dwarf ran back to his mother, weeping and wailing. 'The king wants to kill me,' he said. 'For how can I survive a blow on my head with a bundle of hardwood?'

The old woman told the child not to worry. She gave him two bundles of cogoiol and, placing a tortilla on his head, sent him back to the king.

The king had assembled all his ministers and the nobles of his court for what he hoped would be his triumph over the Dwarf. He took his bundle of wood and hit the Dwarf hard on his head with it. In fact, he hit the Dwarf so hard that the bundle of hardwood splintered into a hundred pieces. But the Dwarf stood unharmed.

Now the King was frightened. He tried to get out of the contest, but the ministers and noblemen insisted he keep his end of the bargain. They insisted the Dwarf hit the king with his bundle of wood.

The Dwarf did so, and at once the king died.

The assembled nobles and ministers and the people of the city who had come to watch the contest declared the Dwarf to be their new king. The old woman's wish had come true—her little child was now a great king.

After this, the old woman disappeared. But it is said, that far away in the village of Mani, there is a deep well leading to an underground passage. In this passage, beside a river and shaded by a great tree, sits an old woman with a serpent by her side. She sells water, but accepts no money. But be careful before you buy her water, for she wants your babies in return, innocent children which her serpent devours.

This old woman is the Dwarf's mother.

Hunahpu and Xbalanque

The stories about the twins Hunahpu and Xbalanque are taken from the *Popol Vuh*, the Council Book of the Quiche Maya people of Guatemala. The *Popol Vuh* was written by the Quiche lords after the Spanish conquest of Central America to preserve as much of their tradition, history and mythology as they could. This is the most exhaustive account of Mayan mythology and tradition that we have today.

The *Popol Vuh* tells of gods and goddesses, and how the world began, and of events that happened before the first true dawn. It foretold of the glory of the Quiche lords in this world, and of the divine twins Hunahpu and Xbalanque.

Xpiyacoc and Xmucane, the oldest among the gods, had

two sons, Hunhunahpu and Vukub-Hunahpu. Hunhunahpu was married to Xbakiyalo and had two sons—Hunbatz and Hunchouen. The whole family loved to play *tlachtli*, a game played with a rubber ball between two teams in great courts where the ball had to be hit by a yoke-shaped device worn on one side of the body. (The remains of several tlachtli courts have been found in the ruins of Mayan cities.)

One day, Hunhunahpu and Vukub-Hunahpu were lured away to Xibalba, the underworld, to play tlachtli, and were tricked, tortured and killed. Xquiq, a princess of Xibalba, however, was pregnant with the children of Hunhunahpu and Vukub-Hunahpu. Her furious father ordered that she be killed. But Xquiq ran away and went to Xmucane, mother of Hunhunahpu and Vukub-Hunahpu.

Xmucane, who was looking after Hunbatz and Hunchouen and grieving for her lost sons, at first refused to accept Xquiq's story. But then she received signs that proved to her that Xquiq was telling the truth.

The Twins and Their Elder Brothers

The twins were born in the mountains and when Xquiq brought them home to their grandmother, the twins were wide awake and crying loudly.

Old Xmucane couldn't bear their crying. 'They're too noisy,' she cried. 'Throw them out!'

So the two children were thrown out of the house. They lived outdoors and grew up outdoors.

This made their older brothers, Hunbatz and Hunchouen, the elder sons of Hunhunahpu, very happy. They were jealous of their little brothers, and didn't want them in the house. They hoped the two boys would die outside.

Now, Hunbatz and Hunchouen were very clever, and also wise for they knew a great many things. They could play the flute and sing, they could write and carve. They could see that their younger brothers would be good and great, but their jealousy made them blind. They hated their younger brothers and wanted them to die.

But Hunahpu and Xbalanque did not die. They grew strong and healthy, and learnt how to hunt and use the blowpipe. Every day they would shoot birds, and bring them to their grandmother to cook.

Xmucane would cook the birds and give them to Hunbatz and Hunchouen. Hunahpu and Xbalanque got nothing. They got no food. They got no love. They only got curses from their older brothers and their grandmother. But they didn't seem to mind. They didn't complain, they didn't grumble. They merely carried on.

One day, Hunahpu and Xbalanque came to their grandmother Xmucane but they didn't bring any birds.

'Why haven't you brought any birds today?' asked Xmucane angrily.

'We have the birds, dear grandmother,' said the twins. 'But they are stuck up in a tree. We shoot the birds but they don't fall. They get stuck in the tree. We can't get them down. So could our elder brothers please come with us to get the birds?'

'We'll come with you in the morning,' said the elder brothers.

Now, Hunahpu and Xbalanque were happy because they had a plot; they had a plan to get rid of their elder brothers. 'Our elder brothers have been cruel to us,' they said to each other. 'Now it is time to get rid of them.'

So next morning, Hunahpu and Xbalanque took their elder brothers to a tree. The tree was full of birds. Hunahpu and Xbalanque started shooting, but not one bird fell out of the tree. The elder brothers watched astonished.

'Oh, the birds get stuck in the tree,' said Hunahpu and Xbalanque. 'Why don't you go up the tree and throw down the birds?'

'Very well,' said the elder brothers, and they climbed the tree.

But as they climbed, the tree began to grow. It grew higher and its trunk grew thicker.

Now the elder brothers wanted to get down, but they couldn't.

'Dear younger brothers,' called Hunbatz and Hunchouen from the tree. 'We can't get down. Tell us how to climb down from this tree because now we're frightened.'

'Oh, take your loincloths off and tie them round your waist like tails,' said Hunahpu and Xbalanque. 'You will find it easier to get down.'

So the elder brothers did that, and suddenly they were turned into monkeys. They went swinging through the branches howling and calling in the trees.

Thus Hunahpu and Xbalanque had their revenge. They got rid of their elder brothers who had been cruel to them. They turned them into monkeys.

Now Hunahpu and Xbalanque went to their grandmother Xmucane and said, 'Something has happened to our elder brothers. They've turned into animals.'

'Don't do anything to your elder brothers, dear grandchildren,' said Xmucane. 'If you have done something to them, I won't be able to bear it.'

'Don't worry, dear grandmother,' said Hunahpu and Xbalanque. 'We'll bring our elder brothers home. But you must promise not to laugh when you see them. Because if you laugh, they will have to go away as animals again.'

Then Hunahpu and Xbalanque started playing their flutes and singing and beating on their drums. Very soon their elder brothers, Hunbatz and Hunchouen, arrived swinging through the trees. The grandmother took one look at their funny faces and long tails and began laughing. She couldn't stop laughing. So the elder brothers went back as they had come, back into the forest.

'Why did you laugh, grandmother?' said Hunahpu and Xbalanque. 'They will never come back if you do. Three times more we will call them, and you must not laugh.'

So Hunahpu and Xbalanque played on their flute and sang and beat on their drums. Their elder brothers came swinging through the trees. And every time the grandmother Xmucane would see their funny faces and their funny antics and would burst out laughing. And every time Hunbatz and Hunchouen would turn around and go back into the forest.

The fourth time that Hunahpu and Xbalanque sang and called to their elder brothers, they did not come. They went far away into the forest and never came back again.

'Don't be sad, grandmother,' said Hunahpu and Xbalanque to Xmucane. 'We are here, we are your grandchildren. Don't feel sad for our elder brothers. They will be remembered. This was their destiny.'

So Hunahpu and Xbalanque began living with their mother and their grandmother. Their elder brothers were remembered for their skill in playing the flute and singing, and for their ability to write and carve. The flautist and singers, writers and carvers of the world, all prayed to Hunbatz and Hunchouen.

But because they had been cruel to their younger brothers, they themselves were humbled.

That had been their destiny.

The Maize Field, the Rat and the Tlachtli Kit

The twins Hunahpu and Xbalanque came into the house to live with their mother Xquiq and their grandmother Xmucane. They had sent away their elder brothers, turned them into monkeys, and now they took their place.

The twins said to Xmucane. 'We'll look after you, grandmother. We have come in place of our elder brothers. Don't worry, grandmother.'

The twins then decided to clear a field for planting maize. They told their mother and grandmother that that is where they were going. 'Bring us our food at midday, grandmother,' they told Xmucane.

Then Hunahpu and Xbalanque took their tools—an axe and a mattock and a hoe. And they put their blowpipes over their shoulders and went off to clear the field.

When they reached the field they had planned to clear, they didn't want to do any work. They only wanted to go hunting with their blowpipes. So they stuck the mattock in the ground, and the axe in a tree. And the mattock and the axe cleared the field. They went through trees and brambles and broke up the ground. And while the tools did all the work, Hunahpu and Xbalanque went hunting with their blowpipes.

But they called to the dove and told her to keep watch. 'When you see our grandmother coming, call out and tell us,' they told the dove.

So the dove sat on a tree and kept watch. When she saw old Xmucane coming, she called out. Hunahpu and Xbalanque ran to pick up their tools. One picked up the axe, one the hoe. They rubbed dirt on their faces and soil on their fingers so that Xmucane would think they had been working all day.

Xmucane brought them their food, and sat there watching them eat. She thought they had been working. She didn't know they had only been hunting. When they had finished eating, Xmucane went away.

When it was night, the twins went home. Their field had been cleared, all ready for planting.

'Oh, dear mother, dear grandmother, we are tired,' said the twins, pretending to be really tired. They yawned and stretched and went straight to bed.

Next morning, when they woke up, they went back to their field of maize. But the field had returned to what it was before their tools had cleared it. Every tree, every bush, ever bramble had grown back just as it used to be before.

'Who has done this to us?' said the twins. 'We must keep watch over our field at night, to see who has done this.'

Their tools cleared the field again. But that night, the twins went home and told their mother and grandmother what had happened, and how the trees and bushes and brambles had grown back in the night. 'We must go back to the field tonight, to find out who did this to us,' the twins said to their mother and grandmother.

Hunahpu and Xbalanque went back to the field and spread a large net to catch whoever had undone their work. Then they hid themselves.

Now, it had been all the animals of the field and the forest who had made the field grow wild again. And in the middle of the night, they came, all the animals great and small. They gathered together in the field and then they sang and made the brambles and bushes and trees grow again.

Hunahpu and Xbalanque tried to catch the animals. First came the jaguar and the puma, but they escaped. Next came the rabbit and the deer, but the twins could only grab their tails, which broke off in their hands. That is why the rabbit and the deer don't have proper tails.

The twins could not catch a single animal. All the animals ran away, except one. The rat got stuck in the net and couldn't get away.

Hunahpu and Xbalanque caught hold of the rat and asked him, 'Why do you undo all our work? Why do you make the trees and bushes and brambles grow again?'

'Will you promise me food if I tell you?' asked the rat.

'We will promise you food if you tell us,' said the twins.

'It is because you are not made for clearing fields and planting,' said the rat. 'You are made for playing tlachtli with your fathers' ball and their kit.' And the rat told them all about their fathers Hunhunahpu and Vukub-Hunahpu, and their adventures in Xibalba and how they died.

The twins felt a great happiness coming over them when they heard of their fathers.

'Can you tell us where their ball and their kit is?' asked the twins.

'Old Xmucane, your grandmother, has them hidden in her roof,' said the rat.

And the rat led them to where Xmucane had hidden her sons' rubber ball and their tlachtli kit. She had hidden them because it was because of the ball game that they had gone to Xibalba and died. She did not want her grandchildren to go the same way.

Hunahpu and Xbalanque thanked the rat and gave him his food, and his food was corn kernels, beans, seeds, cacao. That is why the rat eats these things. 'If you find any of your food that is stored or wasted, eat away, don't stop,' said the twins. So that is why the rat eats stored or wasted food that is his.

When Hunahpu and Xbalanque found their fathers' ball and tlachtli kit, they were happy and began to play. They wanted to play like their fathers, and get an invitation to Xibalba by the lords. But how they managed to do that, and how they managed to trick the dark lords of Xibalba, is another story.

Huitzilopochtli

During the fifteenth and early sixteenth centuries, Central America was dominated by the culture and civilization of a people known to us as the Aztecs. In 1325, the Aztecs founded their city of Tenochtitlan on that spot, the site of modern-day Mexico City. Over the next two hundred years, the Aztecs rose in power and prominence from a small tribe of hunter-gatherers to the rulers of the largest and richest empire in Central America. The civilization was brought to a sudden and complete end by Spanish explorers, who imprisoned the last emperor Moctezuma II in 1519 and destroyed Tenochtitlan in 1521.

Huitzilopochtli was the chief god of the Aztecs. He was the sun god as well as the god of war. The Aztecs believed that it was he who had created their ancestors, given them their language and customs, and assigned them the tasks of fishing and hunting.

Huitzilopochtli's name is derived from the Nahuatl *huitzlin*, which means 'hummingbird', and *opochtli*, which means 'left'. The Aztecs believed that dead warriors were reborn as hummingbirds, and that the south was the left side of the world. So Huitzilopochtli's name can be interpreted to mean 'reborn warrior of the south'.

It was believed Huitzilopochtli was born of the earth goddess Coatlicue on Coatepec the Serpent Mountain, near the city of Tula. He was usually shown as a hummingbird or as a warrior wearing an elaborate headdress of hummingbird feathers. His arms, legs and the lower part of his face were blue; the upper half of his face was black. He carried a shield and a turquoise snake, the Fire Serpent or *xiuhcoatl*. His *nahual*, or animal disguise, was the eagle.

The Aztecs believed that Huitzilopochtli had to be provided with daily nourishment in the form of human hearts and blood. Prisoners captured in battle and slaves were regularly sacrificed in ceremonial rituals. Warriors who were sacrificed thus to the god or who died in battle were called *quauhxicalli*, 'the eagle's people'. It was believed that after their death the warriors became part of the sun's retinue for four years, and then went to live forever in the bodies of hummingbirds.

The title of this story comes from an Aztec hymn to the god, where he says, 'Not in vain did I take the raiment of yellow plumage,/for it is I who makes the sun appear.'

'For It Is I Who Makes the Sun Appear'

Once, under the shadow of Coatepec the Serpent Mountain, near the Toltec city of Tula, there lived a woman called Coatlicue the Serpent-Skirted. Coatlicue had four hundred sons, who were called the Centzon Huitznahua, which means 'four hundred southerners' in Nahuatl. Coatlicue also had one daughter, Coyolxauhqui.

One day, Coatlicue went deep into the mountains to pray. As she prayed, a ball of shining hummingbird feathers fell from the sky into her lap. Fascinated by the brilliant, multicoloured feathers, Coatlicue picked up the ball and tucked it into her bosom for safekeeping. 'Perhaps I should offer these wonderful feathers to the Sun,' she thought.

This was no ordinary ball of feathers, but the soul of a brave warrior who had been killed in battle, and so, sometime later, Coatlicue found that she was going to have another baby. When Coatlicue's sons, the Four Hundred, and her daughter Coyolxauhqui heard this they were furious. 'This new baby must die!' declared Coyolxauhqui, and she urged her brothers to kill the unborn child and their mother.

Coatlicue heard of her children's plans, and she was worried and afraid. But her unborn child reassured her, 'Do not worry, do not fear. They cannot harm us.'

But Coyolxauhqui and the Four Hundred were determined to kill their mother and the unborn child.

They put on their armour and took up their weapons, and with Coyolxauhqui at their head, marched to Coatepec, where Coatlicue waited in fear and anxiety.

But Quauitlicac, one of the Four Hundred, changed his mind. He did not want to kill his mother or her unborn baby. So he left his sister and brothers, and ran ahead to warn Coatlicue.

'Do not be afraid, Brother,' said Coatlicue's unborn baby to Quauitlicac. 'I know exactly what my sister and other brothers plan to do, and I am prepared.'

Quauitlicac, though comforted by the baby's words, could not help worrying. He climbed up to the very top of the mountain to keep watch on the advancing army.

'Brother, keep watch for me, and tell me exactly where the others are,' called out the unborn baby to Quauitlicac.

'They are at Tzompantitlan,' replied Quauitlicac.

A little while later, the baby called out again, 'Brother, now tell me, where are the others?'

'They are at Coaxalco,' said Quauitlicac.

Once more the baby called out, 'Tell me, Brother, where are the others now?'

'They are at Petlac,' said Quauitlicac.

After that the baby and Coatlicue waited in silence, till Quauitlicac called out, 'They are here! Coyolxauhqui and the Centzon Huitznahua! They are on Coatepec!'

And in that instant, Coatlicue's baby sprang out of her womb, fully grown. He was none other than Huitzilopochtli, the sun god in all his glory. He wore hummingbird feathers on his head and his limbs were painted in stripes of blue and black. In his left hand he held his shield of blue, while in his right hand he brandished his special weapon the Fire Serpent. His face—black above and blue below—was terrifying to look at.

With a single blow of the Fire Serpent, Huitzilopochtli shattered Coyolxauhqui into a hundred pieces, which fell far down the mountainside to land on the spot where later Huitzilopochtli's people built his temple. As for the Centzon Huitznahua, they didn't wait for their turn. Instead they turned as one and ran as fast as they could to get away from Huitzilopochtli's fearsome weapon. But Huitzilopochtli ran after them, and chased them round Coatepec four times. Most of the Four Hundred fell into a nearby lake and were drowned. Huitzilopochtli killed all the others with his Fire Serpent, except the few who managed to escape to a place called Uitzlampa where they gave up their weapons and pleaded with Huitzilopochtli for their lives.

Thus was born Huitzilopochtli, the young warrior, the one who makes the sun appear. He created the Aztecs and gave them his secret name, so that they would be his forever, the people of the sun.

The Sons of Abraham

Isaac and Ishmael were the sons of Abraham, the first Hebrew patriarch. Abraham is a figure revered by three great religions: Judaism, Christianity and Islam.

Abraham's story, and that of his sons Isaac and Ishmael, is told in the Book of Genesis of the Old Testament of the Bible. Yahweh, which is Hebrew for 'God', called upon Abraham to leave the city of Ur in Mesopotamia and found a new nation in an unknown land. In return, God promised that Abraham would become the father of many nations.

Abraham's wife Sarah had no children and was now ninety, much past the age of childbearing. But a son was born to her, just as Yahweh had promised.

Ishmael was also Abraham's son, but by Sarah's Egyptian

handmaiden, Hagar. His story is intertwined with that of Isaac.

The Jews and Christians believe that it was Isaac, Abraham's son by his wife Sarah, whom God called upon him to sacrifice. But in Islamic belief, it is Ishmael, or Ismail, who is the favoured son and the one whom Abraham takes for sacrifice. Islamic tradition also says that when Sarah makes Abraham banish Hagar and Ishmael from his house, he takes them to the place that centuries later became the city of Mecca. Hagar's anguish as their water runs out, and the miraculous bubbling of the spring of Zam-Zam are commemorated among the Muslims during the annual pilgrimage of Hajj. The Muslims also believe that Abraham and Ishmael built the Kaaba, their most sacred shrine, which lies near the centre of the Great Mosque of Mecca.

Isaac

Almost four thousand years ago, in the Sumerian city of Ur, there lived a man called Abram and his wife Sarai. Abram and Sarai had no children.

One day, Yahweh, Abram's God, called upon Abram to leave his people and his country, and to go to a land that He would show him, and where Abram would become the father of a new nation. Abram, who was now seventy-five years old, obeyed Yahweh's command without question. He gathered up his cattle and herds of sheep, and together with his wife Sarai travelled to Canaan, the land that lies between Egypt and Syria.

And there Yahweh appeared to Abram and said that He gave the land of Canaan to him and his children, and his children's children, forever.

Abram and Sarai continued to live in Canaan, amid their flocks and the herdsmen and their families. Abram worked hard and prospered so that his herds of cattle and sheep grew in number. Now Abram was an old man of ninety-nine, and his wife Sarai an old woman. They still had no children, and had long given up hope of ever having any.

One day, Yahweh appeared once more to Abram. First He changed Abram's name to 'Abraham', which means 'Father of Many Nations', and Sarai's name to 'Sarah', which means 'princess'. Then God said to Abraham that soon he and Sarah would have a son.

Abraham was so surprised that he laughed. How could he, who was almost hundred, and Sarah, who was ninety, have a child? But Yahweh reassured him, saying that very soon a son would be born to Sarah, and that they should call him Isaac.

Another day, Yahweh appeared to Abraham as he sat outside his tent. Abraham looked up and saw three men standing near him. He welcomed them, and washed their feet, and offered them curds and milk and meat.

'Where is your wife, Sarah?' asked the travellers.

'Inside,' answered Abraham. 'In the tent.'

'Soon she will have a child,' said one of the travellers.

Sarah was listening from inside the tent. 'How can I have a child,' she said to herself. 'I am too old to have babies.' And she laughed in her surprise.

But the traveller asked Abraham. 'Why does Sarah laugh? Is anything too wonderful for God?' And he said once again that soon Sarah would have a child.

As Yahweh had promised, Sarah bore Abraham a son. They called him Isaac, as Yahweh had said.

Sarah was overjoyed. 'Who would ever have thought that I would bear Abraham a son?' she said. 'In my old age, I have found happiness.'

Isaac was brought up tenderly and with great love by his parents. He was everything to Abraham and Sarah.

One day, when Isaac was still a little boy, Yahweh appeared once again to Abraham. 'Abraham!' He called.

Abraham answered his Lord, 'Here I am.'

'Abraham,' said Yahweh. 'Take Isaac, your son, whom you love. Go with him to the land of Moriah, and there offer him as a burnt offering on one of the mountains that I shall show you.' Yahweh was testing Abraham's love for Him. He wanted Abraham to kill his beloved son and offer him as sacrifice to Him.

Abraham silently prepared to do as Yahweh commanded. Early the next morning, he saddled his donkey, called two of his men to accompany him, and taking his son Isaac with him, set off for the distant mountains that Yahweh had told him about.

For three days they travelled, Abraham and Isaac, and

the two young men. Isaac was quite unaware of what was to happen to him, and chattered happily with his father for the entire journey. And after three days, Abraham saw in the distance the mountains.

'Wait here with the donkey,' he told the two young men. 'My son and I will go up into the mountains and offer our worship. And then we shall come back to you.'

Abraham took the wood for the burnt offering that he had brought with him, and gave it to his son Isaac to carry. He himself carried the fire and the knife.

Abraham and Isaac walked on in silence for a while.

Then Isaac said, 'Father?'

'Yes, my son,' said Abraham. 'What is it?'

'We have the fire and the wood for the sacrifice,' said Isaac. 'But where is the lamb?'

'Yahweh Himself will provide the lamb for sacrifice, my son,' said Abraham.

And father and son walked on into the mountains in silence.

Soon they came to the place of sacrifice. There Abraham built an altar, and laid upon it the wood for the fire. Then he took his son Isaac, and laid him on the altar, and tied him up as he would have a lamb. Slowly, then, Abraham reached for his knife to kill his son.

Just then a voice called out, 'Abraham, Abraham.'

'Here I am,' said Abraham.

'Do not do anything to your son,' called the voice, which was that of an angel. 'I know now that you fear God, for you have not withheld anything from Him, not even your beloved son.'

And Abraham looked up and saw a ram, caught by his horns in a thicket. Abraham caught the ram, and offered it as burnt offering to his Lord in place of his son. So Isaac was spared.

And the voice called out a second time and told Abraham that because he had not withheld even his son from his Lord, he would be blessed, and that his children should be as numerous as the stars in the sky and the sand on the seashore, and through them shall all the people on earth be blessed.

And Yahweh fulfilled His promise, for Isaac became the father of Esau and Jacob; and Jacob, later called Israel, had twelve sons, and from his twelve sons came all the tribes of Israel.

Ishmael

Abram, upon the word of Yahweh his God, had moved with his cattle and his sheep, and his wife Sarai, to the land of Canaan. The land had been promised to him and his children, and his children's children forever.

Now, Abram's wife Sarai had no children. Afraid that she may never bear a child, she gave her handmaiden Hagar to Abram to be his wife, so that he may have a child by her. That was the custom in those days.

But when Hagar became pregnant, she began to feel

that she was better than her mistress Sarai. This made Sarai very angry. Sarai complained to Abram about Hagar's behaviour. Abram told Sarai that Hagar was still her handmaiden and that she should deal with her as she saw fit.

However, Hagar, afraid of Sarai's anger, ran away into the wilderness. There, as she rested by a spring, the angel of Yahweh came to her. 'Where have you come from?' the angel asked Hagar. 'And where are you going?'

Hagar explained who she was, and how she had run away from Sarai's anger. The angel reassured her and said, 'You will have a son. He will be called Ishmael.' The angel then asked Hagar to return to Sarai.

Hagar returned to her mistress, and in due course a son was born to her. Abram named him Ishmael, as the angel of Yahweh had predicted. At this time, Abram was already an old man, being eighty-six years of age.

When Abram was almost a hundred years old, Yahweh appeared to him, and changing his name to 'Abraham' and that of his wife Sarai to 'Sarah', told him that he and his wife would soon have a son who would be called Isaac.

Abraham, as he was now called, loved his son Ishmael dearly. 'What will happen to Ishmael?' he wondered. But Yahweh told him that he would not forget Ishmael, who was so beloved of Abraham. 'Ishmael will be the father of twelve nations,' Yahweh promised Abraham.

Soon after, Sarah gave birth to Isaac. Now, though Abraham loved Isaac as well, Sarah was jealous of his love for Ishmael. One day, she saw Ishmael playing with the baby Isaac. Furious, she went to Abraham and said, 'Throw out this slave woman Hagar and her son. Her son shall not be your heir along with mine.'

Abraham was deeply distressed. He loved his son Ishmael and did not want to send him away. But Yahweh appeared to him again and said that he should listen to Sarah. At the same time, Yahweh reassured Abraham that He would look after Ishmael.

So Abraham did as Yahweh said. Early next morning, he gave Hagar some bread and a waterskin for herself and Ishmael, and sent them away. Ishmael was only thirteen years old at this time.

Hagar wandered in the wilderness with her young son, heartbroken and despairing. Soon they had eaten all their bread and drunk all their water. They had nothing left to eat and no water to drink. Hagar looked everywhere for water, but there was not a stream, not a spring, not a well anywhere. Ishmael was weak with hunger, and almost dead with the heat and the lack of water.

At last, Hagar sat Ishmael under a shrub, to shield him from the sun. 'Let me not see my son die,' she said in despair, and weeping, she went and sat far away from him.

But Yahweh heard the child, and His angel called out to Hagar, 'Why do you cry, Hagar? Do not be so sad, for God has seen the boy and heard him. Come, Hagar, lift up your child and hold him close.' Yahweh's angel told again how Ishmael would be the father of a great nation.

Hagar opened her eyes, and saw before her a bubbling spring. She ran to the spring, and filling the waterskin with water, carried it to Ishmael. Slowly, lovingly, she gave him the water to drink, till the child revived.

Yahweh fulfilled his promise. Ishmael grew up in the wilderness. He was very skilled with the bow and arrow. His mother found him an Egyptian bride, and the twelve sons of Ishmael became the fathers of twelve desert tribes.

Maui

The story of Maui is probably the best known of all Polynesian myths and legends. Maui is a demigod, a hero, who is also a trickster, always up to mischief with little regard for social conventions or the right way to behave. His exploits evoke laughter, or sometimes anger and indignation, but at the end, always result in some benefit to mankind.

Maui is credited with such feats as lifting the sky up to its present height, fishing up solid land from the vast ocean that covers the world, and making the sun go slowly in the sky so people have enough daylight to do all that they need to do in a day. Maui is also the one who gave mankind the secret of

Fire, which he obtained from his ancestress Mahuika, through trickery and guile.

Among the Maori people of New Zealand is found the most comprehensive and complete version of the Maui myth.

Maui's Birth

Taranga's child was born early, before his time. He was born by the seashore.

Taranga was afraid of this child who had come into the world before he was fully formed. So she cut off a tuft of her hair and wrapped her baby in it, and then she threw him into the surf and gave him to the waves, to Tangaroa the Ocean.

Tangaroa took the newborn child. The seaweed folded about him and rocked him from side to side, and the breezes that blew carried him back to land, where Tangaroa gave the child up to the sandy shore. There the jellyfish found him, and rolled themselves around him, so that he might be safe. But the flies buzzed round him and the birds gathered round him waiting for him to die as the child lay on the sandy beach. Till the old man Tame-nui-ke-ti-Rangi saw the flies and the birds collected in clusters round the jellyfish. The old man ran as fast as he could, stripped off the jellyfish and found the child within. Then, Tame-nui-ke-ti-Rangi took the child home and hung him up close to the roof of his house so that the child might feel the warm smoke and the heat of the fire.

So the child was saved by the kindness of Tame-nui-ke-ti-Rangi, the wise one.

Maui Finds His Family

Many seasons passed and the baby grew into a child. The child was clever, and now knew as much magic of the earth and the sky as did the wise old Tame-nui-ke-ti-Rangi.

Then one day, Tame-nui-ke-ti-Rangi said to the child, 'Go, find your family. Your time with me has ended.'

So he left Tame-nui-ke-ti-Rangi.

He travelled all day and all night, and when the land was too difficult to cross, he turned into a bird and flew. In this way, he at last found his mother, his relations and his brothers, one night when they were all dancing in the Great House of Assembly.

The little child crept into the Great House of Assembly, and there were his four brothers, sitting. He crept behind them and sat down with them, so that when their mother Taranga came to get her children for the dance, she found one more. She counted aloud, 'One, that's Maui-taha; two—that's Maui-roto; three—that's Maui-pae; four —that's Maui-waho.' And then she saw another little one.

'Another one!' said Taranga. 'Where has this fifth one come from?' she asked.

Then the little child said, 'I'm your child too. I'm Maui-the-baby.'

Then Taranga counted them all over again, 'Maui-taha, Maui-roto, Maui-pae, Maui-waho. That's all. That's four. There should be only four of you. Who is this fifth one? Who are you?'

But little Maui said again, 'I'm your child too. I am Maui-the-baby.'

Now Taranga got angry. 'Come—you are no child of mine. You must belong to someone else. Leave this house at once!'

Then little Maui said, 'Very well. I will leave if you say so. But I must be your child. I was born by the seashore, and you threw me, wrapped in your hair, into the waves. And Tangaroa looked after me, the seaweed rocked me, and the breezes blew me to shore, and Tame-nui-ke-ti-Rangi took me to his house and hung me up near the roof so I would stay warm. And then I grew and heard of this Great House and came to find you. I know my brothers from the time I was inside you.' And little Maui recited all the names of his brothers. 'This is Maui-taha, and this is Maui-roto, and this is Maui-pae, and this is Maui-waho. And I am Maui-the-baby.'

When Taranga heard him talk like this, she believed him, and she opened her arms to him and held him. 'You are my son, my little son, my last-born child,' she cried. And she called him Maui-tikitiki-a-Taranga, which means 'Maui-formed-in-the-topknot-of-Taranga'. And from then on that was his name.

Now Taranga called to Maui and said, 'Come, my little child, come sleep with me, your mother, so that I may kiss you and cuddle you.' And little Maui ran to his mother and slept with her at night.

When his brothers saw this they were jealous. 'Our mother never calls us to sleep with her,' they said. 'We are the children she has seen growing up, but never has she called to us to sleep with her so that she may cuddle us. So why is she calling this little stranger, who may not even be her child?'

But the two eldest ones said, 'Never mind if our mother calls him to her. Let us be kind to him, and let him be our little brother. It is better to be kind and to share all we have than to fight amongst us. So let us be kind to the little fellow, and let him be our little brother.'

The other brothers heard this and agreed that it was better to be kind than to fight. 'Yes, yes, you are right,' they said. 'Let our jealousy finish here.'

And so the brothers of little Maui looked upon him as their little brother.

That night, little Maui slept cuddled up with his mother Taranga. But in the morning, very early, up rose Taranga, and went away before her children were awake. The five boys woke up and looked all around, but they could not see her.

The four elder brothers were used to this, so they didn't bother. But little Maui was very unhappy. 'I can't see her anywhere,' he said. 'Maybe she has gone to make some food for us,' he thought. But Taranga had gone far away.

When night fell, Taranga came back. Once again she called to little Maui, 'Come, my child, come sleep with me tonight.' So Maui cuddled up with his mother and went to sleep. But when he woke up in the morning, his mother had disappeared again. Little Maui was very unhappy again.

This kept happening for some time—every night Taranga would come back to her children, and in the morning, she would vanish. At last, little Maui decided to find out where his mother went every morning.

So one night, as his mother slept and his four brothers slept as well, Maui woke up and stole his mother's apron, and her belt and all her clothes and hid them. Then he shut the door and window tight, and blocked up every little crevice and chink, so that the light of the dawn could not get into the house and wake his mother.

Soon the morning came, but no light came into the house. Maui's mother and his brothers slept on. The sun rose slowly in the sky, till it was bright daylight outside, and still his mother and his brothers slept on. Till at last his mother woke up and said to herself, 'What kind of night is this that it does not end?' Then she realized her clothes were gone, and jumping up started searching for her clothes, her apron, her belt. But she couldn't find them. She saw that the door and window had been blocked too. So she ran and pulled out the things with which the door and window had been blocked. And then she saw the sun was high in the sky and that it was broad daylight.

Then Taranga was deeply distressed. She pulled on an old cloak, and pulling open the door, ran out.

As soon as his mother ran out of the house, Maui jumped up and peeped out through the door of the house. He saw his mother reaching down and pulling up a tuft of grass, and then dropping down into a hole underneath it. She clapped the tuft of grass back into the hole, as though it were a lid, and vanished. Maui ran to the spot where she had disappeared and pulled up the same tuft of grass. Peering into the hole that opened, he saw a long underground passage running deep into the earth.

Maui ran back to the house and woke up his brothers. 'Wake up, wake up,' he called. 'See, our mother has disappeared again.' And he told them all about the hole in the grass that Taranga had vanished into. 'Where do you think our mother and our father live?' little Maui then asked his brothers.

'How can we know, we've never seen it,' answered his elder brothers. 'And why should we care? And why should *you* care? We are happy here. Can you not be happy here with us?'

But little Maui was not happy. He wanted to know where his mother and his father lived.

'Well, then, you will have to go alone and try to find our mother and father,' said the brothers.

So Maui used all the magic he had learnt and turned himself into a beautiful pigeon. Then off he flew, into the long underground passage into which his mother had gone. On flew Maui the Pigeon, on and on. Sometimes the passage became very narrow, and sometimes it was wide and beautiful. But at last, in the distance, he saw a grove of *manapau* trees and under these trees some people.

Maui flew straight on, till he came to the grove. He perched on the tree under which the people sat. And there he saw his mother, with a man who was his father. The other people called to them by name, and then Maui was sure he had found his mother and his father.

So he hopped down lower, and with his beak, pecked off one of the berries that grew on the tree. He dropped the berry gently so that it struck his father. His father brushed it off. 'It was nothing,' he said to Maui's mother. 'Just a berry that fell by chance.'

Then Maui pecked off more berries and began throwing them down hard, so that they struck both his mother and his father. They looked up, and all the people jumped up, looking into the tree to see who was throwing the berries. And they saw Maui the Pigeon. Then the people began to pelt the pigeon with stones to make it fly away, but they couldn't hit it.

Then Maui's father picked up a stone and threw it at the pigeon. It struck him on the left leg and the pigeon fell down, fluttering and flapping. Now, Maui had wished that his father's stone would hit him—so it had. Otherwise no stone could have hit him.

The people ran to pick the fluttering bird up, but the bird changed into a boy. And the people were frightened. 'No wonder he did not fly off,' cried some of them.

'It was a boy all along!'

'No,' said the others. 'More likely a god—just look at him, we have never seen anyone look like him.'

'I see one who looks like him every night that I visit my children,' said Taranga. And then she told her friends and her husband the story of little Maui-the-baby.

Then Taranga turned to Maui and asked him, 'Where do you come from? From westward?'

And Maui answered, 'No.'

Then Taranga asked again, 'From the north-east? From the south-east, then? From the south?'

And Maui answered, 'No.'

Then Taranga asked, 'Was it the wind that blows that brought you here, then?'

And Maui answered, 'Yes.'

'This is indeed my child,' cried Taranga. 'Are you Maui-taha?'

'No,' said Maui.

'Are you Maui-tikitiki-a-Taranga?'

'Yes,' answered Maui.

And Taranga embraced him and welcomed him. Then, Maui's father, whose name was Makea-tu-tara welcomed him and took him to cleanse him from all impurities and perform the sacred rituals, so that the gods would keep Maui safe.

So Maui discovered where his mother and his father lived.

Muyingwa, a Hummingbird and Two Children

In the south-western part of the USA, in northern Arizona, there rise three stand-alone hills with flat tops: the First, Second and Third Mesas. The Hopis have lived in this area for more than a thousand years. The village of Old Oraibi, mentioned in the story below, is on the Third Mesa, and is probably the oldest continuously inhabited village in the US.

A very long time ago, the people of Oraibi had nothing to eat because it had not rained for many years. The corn could not grow, and after a while the people had eaten all of the corn they had saved from previous years. People began to move away from Oraibi. Soon everyone had left the village, except for two little children, a little boy and his sister.

One day, the little boy made a little bird from the pith of a sunflower stalk, and gave it to his little sister to play with. The boy then went away to look for food for both of them.

His little sister played all day with the little bird, throwing it up into the air as though to make it fly. Suddenly, the bird came to life, and becoming a real hummingbird, flew away.

A little later, the boy came back. He had found nothing to eat.

'Where is the bird I made for you to play with?' the boy asked his sister.

'It flew away,' said his sister.

The children slept hungry that night. There was nothing for them to eat. But in the morning, the little bird came back, and flew into an opening in one of the walls.

'My little bird has come back!' cried the girl in amazement.

'Where is it?' asked her brother, equally amazed.

'It went into that opening, there,' said the little girl pointing. Her brother carefully put his hand into the opening in the wall. The opening seemed very large inside. The boy felt around carefully, but he couldn't find the bird. Instead he found a little ear of corn.

The boy drew out the ear of corn, and the children broke it into two, roasted it and ate it.

After a while, the bird hopped out of the opening and flew away again. The next day it returned with a larger ear of corn. This too the children broke into two, roasted and ate. Once again the little bird flew away, to return the following day with a still larger ear of corn for the children. It did this for four days. On the fifth day, the bird came back as usual, but did not bring any corn with it. It flew into its opening in the wall and vanished.

The boy carefully put his hand into the opening, and this time drew out the little bird. But the bird was no longer a real hummingbird. It had turned back into the little toy he had made for his sister to play with.

The boy took the bird carefully in his hand and said, 'You are a living bird. You must go and hunt for our parents. They have left us here, all alone, and perhaps you can find them for us. Also bring us something to eat, because we are hungry and have no food. Fly south, and look for our mother and our father, and bring them back to us.'

But the boy could not make the bird fly. So he turned to his sister and asked her how she had made it fly. The little girl took the bird by the wings and threw it up in the air. 'This is how I did it,' she said. At once, the bird came alive again, and turning into a real hummingbird, flew away.

A little south of Oraibi, at a place called Tu'wanashabe,

the bird saw a cactus plant with a single red flower. At once the bird flew to the cactus plant, and removing it, saw beneath it an opening. The bird entered the opening and found itself in a *kiva* with herbs and grasses growing in it.

Now, kivas were the large underground chambers used by the Hopis for meetings, the walls were richly decorated with beautiful mural paintings.

At the north end of this kiva was another opening. Flying through the opening, the bird found itself in another kiva. Here it found some corn, with pollen on it, and ate some of it.

At the north end of this second kiva was another opening. Flying through this, the bird found itself in another kiva, which was full of grass and herbs and corn of all kinds. Here also lived Muyingwa, god of growth and germination.

This last kiva was also full of birds of various kinds, including hummingbirds. It was the hummingbirds who first noticed the little bird and told Muyingwa about it. 'Somebody has come in,' they said to Muyingwa.

'Who is it?' asked Muyingwa. 'Where is he? Let him come here.'

So the little bird fluttered on to Muyingwa's arm and waited for him to speak.

'What are you doing here?' Muyingwa asked the little bird.

'What are *you* doing here?' asked the little bird. 'Why have you come down here, not bothering about the people up there? Your fields up there look very bad. It has not rained for five years and nothing is growing any more. All the people have left, except for two poor little children who are the only ones left in Oraibi. They have nothing to eat. You come back up there and make things better.'

'All right,' answered Muyingwa. 'I will think about the matter.'

The little bird then asked for something to eat for itself, and something to take to the two little children. 'They are hungry,' said the little bird. 'They have not eaten all day.'

Muyingwa told the bird to take anything it wanted for itself and the children. So the bird broke off a large ear of corn and flew back with it to the children and left the corn in the opening in the wall as before.

The children were very happy to see the little bird again. They drew out the ear of corn and shared it between them as before. The children turned to the bird, which still sat in the opening, and thanked it for its kindness. 'We can still live here because of you,' they said to the bird. 'You bring us food, so we stay alive. You must never go away.'

The bird promised to stay close by. 'I will stay at Tu'wanashabe,' it said.

The children then asked the bird to find their parents, and the bird flew off to hunt for them. It flew over the fields of Oraibi, and finally it came to a place called Toho. There it found the mother and father of the two little children. The father and mother had found some cactus plants to eat, and that is what they were living on. They were thin and weak without proper food.

The children's hummingbird flew past them so quickly that they could not see it. The father felt something and said, 'Something passed by here.' But when the parents looked around, they could not see anything. The hummingbird flew back, and this time the parents of the children saw it. 'Who are you, flying about here?' the man asked the bird. The bird stopped flying about, though it kept its wings beating and hovered in the air, listening to what the children's father had to say. The father told the bird how the people had nothing to eat, and how they were starving, and begged the bird to show them where to find food.

But the bird flew away to the children. 'Did you find our parents?' asked the children. 'Yes,' replied the bird. 'I found them near Toho.' And the bird flew away again to find the children something to eat.

Meanwhile, Muyingwa had been thinking about what the hummingbird had said to him. At last, he decided to go back up into the world and set things right there. He moved into the first kiva above him—it rained a little in Oraibi then. He then moved up into the next kiva, and it rained a little more—and when he finally came out of the last kiva, he found the herbs and grasses were growing nicely.

The children's parents had seen the clouds over Oraibi from a distance, and seen the rain. They decided to return to their village, not even hoping to find their children alive. Slowly, the other people of Oraibi who had left, but had not yet died from hunger, also saw the rain over Oraibi and returned to their village. The children found their parents again, and when they grew up, they, and then their descendants, became chiefs and important people in the village of Oraibi.

This story is still told among the Hopi Indians, of the two children, and their hummingbird and Muyingwa. Some of the details have been forgotten over the centuries—so perhaps the story used to be longer.

The Pleiades and the Pine Tree

The Cherokee peoples used to live around the Great Lakes and later in the south-eastern USA. After much persecution and discrimination after the formation of the USA in 1776, the Cherokees were forced to move to north-eastern Oklahoma.

The Cherokees have several beautiful stories explaining the origin of the world and the creatures in it. This story, and the one following it, are two of these.

Long ago, when the world was still new and did not have in it all the things it has today, there lived seven young boys. The boys spent all their time playing the gatayusti game, which is a game played by rolling a stone wheel along the ground and striking it with a curved stick. All day long the boys would play gatayusti, never stopping, never doing anything else, never working in the cornfields.

Their mothers scolded the boys. 'Stop your game,' they would say. 'Go and work in the cornfields like the other boys.' But these seven boys never listened and never stopped playing the gatayusti game.

One day, the mothers were really fed up. They collected some gatayusti stones and boiled them along with the corn for the boys' dinner. When the boys came home hungry after playing the gatayusti game all day, their mothers fished out the gatayusti stones from the pot and served them to the boys. 'You like gatayusti better than the cornfields,' scolded the mothers. 'Now eat gatayusti for your dinner instead of corn!'

At this, the boys became really angry. They went off, all together, to the place where they played their gatayusti game. 'We'll go away,' they said to each other. 'We'll go away to a place where we will never bother them again.' And slowly the boys began to dance, round and round in a circle, praying to the spirits to help them get away.

The mothers of the boys waited, thinking their sons would be back once their anger had cooled, but the boys did not come back. At last, the mothers went out to look for their sons. They saw them dancing, round and round in a circle, praying to the spirits to help them get away. And as the mothers watched, they saw that their sons' feet were no longer touching the earth. With every circle that they completed, the boys rose higher in the air.

The mothers ran towards their sons, to stop them from flying away altogether. But it was too late. By that time the boys had risen so high that their mothers could not reach them. All except one boy, whose mother managed to pull him down with the help of a gatayusti pole. But this boy fell to the ground so hard that he sank into the earth and vanished.

The six boys who were left rose higher and higher till they reached the sky and were turned into stars. We call them the Pleiades, but the Cherokees still call them 'Ani'tsutsa', which means 'The Boys'. Their people mourned and grieved over the boys for a long time, but they remained shining far up in the sky.

And the mother whose son had vanished into the earth wept the longest. Every day she would sit by the spot where her son had vanished and weep tears of grief and sorrow into the earth. Till one day a little green shoot peeped out of the earth. The mother watered the little shoot with her tears, and slowly it grew into a tall and stately tree. We call this tree the Pine.

And the Pleiades and the Pine tree are of one kind and both shine with the same light even to this day.

The Bears

This is another Cherokee story about how things came to be.

Long ago, when the world was new, there lived a Cherokee clan called Ani-Tsa'guhi. In one family of this clan there was a boy with whom this story begins.

This boy used to love the mountains. He would leave his home and go up into the mountains whenever he could, and stay as long as he could. Soon he began going up into the mountains every day, and staying longer and longer. He would leave his house at dawn, and go up into the mountains, and not come back till it was dark. Very soon he even stopped eating at home.

Now his parents began to worry. They told him not to go up into the mountains that often and for so long, but he would not listen. They scolded him, but still he did not listen. He continued going up into the mountains every day.

After a while, his parents noticed that he was beginning to look different—long, brown hair had begun to grow all over his body. His parents were really concerned. They wondered what was wrong with their boy. So they took him aside and asked him why he stayed up in the mountains that long, and why he had stopped eating at home.

'It is much better up in the mountains than here,' answered the boy. 'I get plenty to eat there, and the food is far better than the corn and beans we eat at home. Very soon I am going to go up into the mountains forever and never come back down.'

'Don't do that, son!' cried his parents. 'Don't leave us forever. Don't go up into the mountains.'

But the boy insisted that it was much better in the mountains. 'You can see that I am different now, I have become used to the life in the mountain forests,' said the boy. 'Very soon I will not be able to live here. And if you are wise, you will not stop me. Instead, you will come with me into the mountains, for life is easier there.' And the boy explained how there was always plenty to eat in the mountain forests, and how no one had to work for food. 'But,' added the boy, 'if you want to come with me into the mountains, you must fast for seven days.'

The boy's parents talked the matter over amongst themselves, then went to the headman of their clan. They explained to the headman all that their son had said. The headman called a council of their clan, and everyone talked the matter over. At the end, it was decided that the clan would go with the boy into the mountains. 'Here we have to work very hard,' said everyone. 'There is never enough to eat. But in the mountain forests, the boy says, there is plenty of food available for everyone. So we will go with him.' And so the Ani-Tsa'guhi fasted for seven days, and on the morning of the seventh day, the boy led the way into the mountains and all the Ani-Tsa'guhi followed him.

The other clans saw the Ani-Tsa'guhi leave and were sad. They sent messengers to stop them and to ask them to come back to their village. But the Ani-Tsa'guhi would not turn back. 'We are going where there is always plenty to eat,' they said. 'From now on we shall be called yanu, or bears.' And the messengers saw that long, brown hair was growing all over the bodies of the Ani-Tsa'guhi. Since they had not eaten human food for seven days they were no longer human—they were changing.

And the Ani-Tsa'guhi continued, 'When you yourselves

are hungry, come into the forests and call us, and we shall come. We shall give you our own flesh to eat. Do not be afraid to kill us for we can never die.' And the Ani-Tsa'guhi taught the messengers the songs they should sing to call them in the forest.

When the songs were over, the Ani-Tsa'guhi started off once again for the mountains while the messengers turned back to their villages.

And the messengers told their people later, how, after they had gone a little way, they looked back and saw a herd of bears going into the mountain forests.

How the Winds Came to Be

The Aleuts are natives of the Aleutian Islands and of western Alaska. They are closely related to the Inuits in language, race and culture.

The cold hostile world of the Aleuts, covered in snow and ice for most of the year, is reflected in the story. Igaluk is the Moon Spirit in Aleutian belief. Among the Inuits, he is the moon god.

Long ago, there was a time when the world was still new. In that time there were no winds. Everything was still.

In a little village by the mouth of the Yukon, there lived a man and his wife. The man and his wife had everything in the world to make them happy, but they did not have a child. 'If only we had a child,' they would sigh.

'If it were a son, I would teach him to hunt seals and whales,' the man would say. 'We would walk over the ice, and set traps and snares.'

'And if it were a daughter, I would teach her to weave the finest baskets in the world,' the woman would sigh.

And so the man and his wife wished for a child.

One night, as the woman lay fast asleep, she had a dream. She dreamt that a sledge, pulled by dogs, drew up at her door. The driver of the sledge called out to her, and beckoned that she should ride with him. The woman climbed into the sledge, and all at once the sledge rose up, up into the dark night sky.

The sledge flew faster and faster, through the black sky. The snow-covered earth shone white beneath, and the stars twinkled bright above. But the woman was not afraid, because she knew that the driver of the sledge must be Igaluk, the Moon Spirit, who comforts those who are sad.

All at once, the sledge came down to earth and stopped. The world lay still and silent. There was nothing to be seen in all that white and glittering plain of snow and ice, except for a small tree that grew out of the frozen ground.

'Look,' said Igaluk pointing at the tree with his whip. 'Take that tree, and make of it a child. And you will find happiness.'

Before the woman could ask him more, or question him, Igaluk vanished, and the woman awoke to find herself in her own warm bed.

The woman kept thinking of what she had dreamt. The dream had been so real that the woman believed that Igaluk had in truth come down to her. She woke up her husband, and told him about her dream. 'Go,' said the woman. 'Go at once to find the tree that Igaluk showed me.'

The husband grumbled at being woken up like this. 'It was only a dream,' he said. 'And it's the middle of the night right now!'

But the woman insisted. 'Igaluk himself came down to me,' she said. 'You must go now to find that tree.'

At last, the husband got out of bed, and putting on his warmest furs and shouldering his axe, walked out in search of the tree. As he came to the edge of the village, he saw before him a path, lit as if by moonlight, and leading straight ahead. The man then knew that Igaluk the Moon Spirit was showing him the way. Now believing in his wife's dream, he followed the moonlit path over the snow till at last he came to the very tree his wife had seen in her dream. The man took his axe and cut down the tree, and carried it home.

Next day, in the evening, the man carved a little boy out of the tree. His wife made little sealskin clothes for the wooden child and lovingly dressed him in them. Out of the remaining wood, the man carved a tiny spear and a tiny knife, and a set of little wooden spoons and dishes. He set the weapons in front of the wooden child, while his wife filled the tiny dishes with food and water and placed them by the child as well.

The man and his wife then went to sleep.

In the middle of the night, the woman was woken by a strange sound. She looked around and what did she see? The little wooden child was alive! It had eaten all the food, and drunk all the water. The woman woke her husband and the couple ran to the child and hugged him and called him their son. After a while, they carefully put the tiny child to bed and went to sleep again themselves.

In the morning when they awoke, they found that their child had gone, as had his spear and knife. They could see his tiny footsteps in the snow, leading out of the village. But suddenly the tracks stopped, and there was no trace of the child. The couple hunted high and low in the snow and ice for their child, but they could not find him. Weary and heartbroken, they returned home.

Now, though the man and his wife did not know it, the child had taken the same moonlit path as his father the night before. On and on went the child, along the path lit by Igaluk the Moon Spirit himself. At last, the child came to the eastern edge of the world, where the sky touches the earth.

And there the child saw an opening in the sky wall, covered over with a piece of skin. The covering bulged as though something was pushing at it from the outside. Curious, the child took his tiny knife, and cut the cords that kept the skin covering in place.

All at once a great wind rushed in, bringing with it animals and birds. The child let the wind blow for a while, and then covering up the opening in the sky wall, said:

Blow, Wind, blow,
Sometimes strong,
Sometimes slow,
Sometimes do not blow.

And securing the cover firmly in place, the child went on his way.

After a while he came to the southern edge of the world, and there found another opening in the sky wall, covered up with a piece of skin and bulging as before. He slashed the cords that held the covering in place, and in poured a warmer wind, bringing with it more animals, birds and bushes. After a while, the child covered up the opening, saying to the wind as before:

Blow, Wind, blow,
Sometimes strong,
Sometimes slow,
Sometimes do not blow.

At the western edge of the world, the child found a similar opening. When he removed the cover, in poured a wind with rain and storm. The child quickly covered up the hole, and instructing the wind as before, went on his way.

Finally, he came to the northern edge of the world, where it was immensely cold. Here too he found the hole in the sky wall, covered up with a piece of skin. As soon as the child opened the hole, in whistled a furious gale, howling and blowing and whirling snow and ice. The child quickly covered up the hole, and instructing the wind as before, went on his way.

The child now moved inwards, away from the sky wall, and to the very centre of the earth. There he saw the sky, arching over the earth like a vast canopy. Now he was sure that he had travelled everywhere and seen all that he needed to.

So he decided to return to the village from where he had come, home to his parents. The man and his wife were overjoyed to see him, for they had given up all hope. The child told them all about his travels, and how he had let the winds into the world.

With the winds came the birds of the air and the animals of the land. The winds stirred up the sea so that seals and whales and walruses could be found all along the coast. Hunting was easy and food was plentiful. The people of the village honoured the wooden child for the happiness he had brought them, just as Igaluk the Moon Spirit had said he would.

Ever afterwards, the Aleut people make wooden dolls for their children, knowing that happiness will come to those who care for them.

The Children of the Sun and the Moon

The Yoruba people live in the south-western Nigeria. At one time, they were organized into several kingdoms, each ruled by the oba or king. Traditionally, they believed in almost 400 gods, goddesses and spirits, most with their own cults and priests. They also have an extensive literature of poetry, myth, stories and proverbs. This story tells of how there came to be stars in the sky and fish in the sea.

Long ago, the Sun and the Moon were married to each other.

The Sun would sail across the sky, blazing in all his glory, till he would reach the end of the world where Sky and Earth meet. At night, when his light would be hidden, his wife the Moon would sail gently across the sky, till the Sun rose again in the morning.

The Sun and the Moon had many children. The boys were like their father the Sun, already blazing with light, even though they were little. The girls were like their mother the Moon, glowing softly.

Now, the young suns greatly admired their father and wanted to be like him. They too wanted to sail across the sky down to the end of the world where Sky and Earth met. But their father would not take them with him.

So one day, the young suns gathered together in a body, and began following their father as he started off on his journey across the sky.

'Go back!' ordered the Sun. 'You may not follow me! There is place for only one Sun in the sky!'

But the young suns replied, 'We want to be like you! We too want to sail across the sky all day!'

The Sun again ordered his sons to return home to their mother, but the boys would not listen. They insisted on following him.

At this, the Sun grew angry, and also afraid—he felt that

the brilliance of his sons might outshine him very soon. So, in anger and fear, he turned upon his sons and tried to kill them.

The young suns ran in fright and took refuge with their grandmother Yemaja, the goddess of brooks and streams. Yemaja, to save her grandchildren from the wrath of the Sun, turned them into fish and hid them in the sea and the rivers and streams of the earth.

But the daughters of the Sun and the Moon had remained quietly at home with their mother. They are still there with her, and we can see them following the Moon at night, when the Sun's fierce light is hidden.

And so there came to be fish in the sea and the rivers and streams; and also stars in the sky.

Cuchulainn

The Celts were an ancient people who live in Europe at least as far back as the second millennium BCE. By about the first century BCE, Celtic tribes and groups were found from Britain in the west to Anatolia in the east, and were later partly absorbed into the ancient Roman Empire as Gauls, Boii, Galatians, and Celtiberians. Celtic languages are still spoken in Ireland, Highland Scotland, Wales and Brittany.

The mythology of the Celts of Ireland and Great Britain is well preserved. In Wales and Cornwall are found the stories of King Arthur, mythical hero and king, who some say, is not dead but only asleep, and who will awake when his people have need of him. In Ireland are found many myths and legends telling of gods and heroes, and the great kings and queens that have been. One such hero is the young Cuchulainn.

The adventures of Cuchulainn (pronounced Cou-hou-linn) are spread across seventy-six tales contained in the collection of stories known as the Ulster cycle, which tell of the Ulaidh, the ancient people from whom the province of Ulster got its name. Cuchulainn's real father is Lug, god of light, and master of all crafts.

His most famous exploits are related in the twenty tales that make up the central saga in the Ulster cycle—the *Táin Bó Cuailnge: The Cattle Raid of Cooley*. This is the story of the long war waged by the men of Connaught under their queen Medb (pronounced Mev) against the men of Ulster under Conchobar.

How Cuchulainn Came to Conchobar's Court

In the days when King Conchobar mac Nessa ruled, there was born to Dechtire the king's sister, a little baby son whom she called Setanta. Setanta later came to be known as Cuchulainn.

As a small child in his parents' house, Setanta would listen with wonder and fascination to stories about King Conchobar and his knights. He also heard stories of the boys at Conchobar's court at Emain, who spent their time playing hurley and other games of skill, waiting for the day when they would be men and knights and warriors under Conchobar. And Setanta longed to go to Emain, to join the boy-troop of Conchobar.

So he told his mother Dechtire, that he longed to go to the playing fields of Emain.

'It is too soon for you, my son,' said Dechtire. 'Wait till you are older, or there comes someone who can take you with him and look after you.'

'That would take too long, my mother,' said Setanta. 'I will not wait that long. You must tell me where Emain lies and I will find my way there.'

'It lies to the north, my son,' said Dechtire. 'It is too far for you to go, and the way is difficult and dangerous. The Sliab Fuait, the Few Mountains, lie between you and Emain.'

'I must go to Emain, my mother,' said Setanta. 'Never mind how long or difficult the journey, I must go.'

So little Setanta, who was only five years old, set forth all by himself for Emain, the court of his uncle, King Conchobar. With him he took his toys to play with on the way. He took his hurley of bronze and his ball of silver, and his little staff and his little shield and his toy darts.

To shorten his journey, he played with his toys: he would hit the ball a good long distance with his hurl-bat, then throw the hurley after it; he'd throw his toy darts, and his toy staff the same long distance, then run as fast as he could after them. And he would snatch up the hurl-bat and pick up the ball and gather up the toy darts, all before his toy staff hit the ground. Then he would do it all over again. In this way, playing with his toys, little Setanta reached Emain.

There, on the green, he saw the boy-troop at play with their hurl-bats and their ball, under the leadership of Folloman, Conchobar's son. Without waiting to introduce himself, or ask for permission to join, little Setanta ran on to the green, and capturing the ball, drove it straight towards the goal. No one could take the ball from him or stop him.

The boys stared at him in amazement, and also in anger. 'How dare the little brat spoil our game?' said Folloman, the king's son. 'Besides, he has joined in without first asking for our protection.' In Emain, it was forbidden to join in the games of the boys of the boy-troop without first asking for their protection. 'Come, boys,' called Folloman. 'Let us teach this young fellow a lesson for breaking in on our game this way.'

There were a hundred and fifty young boys in the boy-troop of Emain. A hundred and fifty of them ran at Setanta all together, and threw their hundred and fifty bats at his head. He fended them off with his toy staff. They threw their hundred and fifty balls at him. He fended them off with his hands. They threw their hundred and fifty toy spears at him. He fended them off with his toy shield.

And then a great anger came over little Setanta. He shuddered and shook and his hair seemed on fire. One eye became as small as a needle's eye, while the other opened as wide as the mouth of a wine cup. His mouth stretched from ear to ear, and his whole body was covered in a furious light. Then little Setanta ran among the boys of the boy-troop of Conchobar and scattered them. Fifty of them fell to the ground under Setanta's anger, while the rest ran for safety as fast as they could.

Close by sat King Conchobar, playing chess with one of his knights. 'Hold still, little fellow,' said Conchobar, catching hold of Setanta by the wrist as he ran past. 'You are not treating my boy-troop very gently, are you?'

'And I have good reason not to,' said little Setanta. 'They haven't been very gentle with me, when all I wanted was to play with them. I did not know you treated guests so harshly.'

'Who are you, little fellow?' asked Conchobar.

'Setanta, I am,' said Setanta. 'Son of Sualtim, and your own sister Dechtire.'

'Did you not know that it is forbidden among the boys of the boy-troop of Emain to join in their game without first seeking their protection?' asked Conchobar.

'No,' said little Setanta. 'I did not know, otherwise I would have been on my guard against them.'

At that, Conchobar called out to the boys, 'Here, you boys! Do you grant your protection to little Setanta, my sister's son?'

And the boys all gathered together and cried, 'Yes—we grant it.'

But Setanta once more ran into the boys and started fighting them, and laid fifty of them flat on the ground before Conchobar could stop him.

'Hey, little fellow!' cried Conchobar. 'Why are you still fighting the boys?'

'They must come under my protection as I have come under theirs,' said Setanta. 'Otherwise I will fight every one of them, till they are all laid flat on the ground.'

At that Conchobar said to him, 'Do you, little boy, grant your protection to the boys of the boy-troop?'

And Setanta said, 'Yes—I grant it.'

From that moment, the boy-troop came under the protection and shield of little Setanta, who was only five years old, but who had already shown signs of greatness.

And that was how Setanta came to live at the court of Conchobar and become one of the boys of the boy-troop of Emain.

How Cuchulainn Was Named

There lived in Ulster the smith Culainn, chief smith of King Conchobar. Once Culainn invited Conchobar to his home for a feast. Conchobar accepted the invitation, and when the time came for the feast, set off for Culainn's home with a few chosen men.

On his way, Conchobar passed the green of Emain where the boy-troop were playing. And he saw the most amazing sight: a single boy was ranged against the remaining hundred and fifty, and winning every single goal and game. Conchobar watched the boy with wonder and amazement.

This boy was no other than little Setanta, the six-year-old son of Conchobar's sister.

Conchobar was so pleased with what he saw that he called Setanta to him and said, 'Little boy, come with us to the feast to which we go, for you shall be a guest with us.'

But Setanta answered, 'No, I cannot come to the feast with you. The boys haven't finished their game as yet, and I will not go till we have played enough.'

'That will take a long time,' said the king. 'And we cannot wait that long.'

'Carry on without me,' said Setanta, 'and I will follow you to the feast.'

'But you do not know the way,' said the king.

'I will follow the trail left by your horses and chariots,' said Setanta.

So, leaving little Setanta to finish his game with the other boys, and to follow them later to the feast, Conchobar and his men carried on to the house of Culainn the smith.

Culainn received the king and his men with great honour. Fresh rushes were spread on the floor for them, and food and wine provided. Soon the king and his men were eating and drinking and having a wonderful time.

When the feast was under way, Culainn went up to Conchobar and asked, 'O Conchobar, have you asked anyone to follow you to this feast tonight?'

'No,' said Conchobar, 'I have not.' He had forgotten all

about little Setanta whom he had invited to accompany him and who was supposed to follow later.

'Why do you want to know?' asked Conchobar of Culainn.

And the smith answered, 'I have a dog, a mighty and ferocious hound brought all the way from Spain. When I set him loose he lets no stranger approach my house, and I and all in it are safe. The dog knows no one but me, and will tear into pieces anyone who approaches. So I ask, before I set the dog free, does anyone follow you here tonight?'

When Conchobar said once again that no one was supposed to follow him, Culainn went outside and set his huge dog free, to guard the house. The dog lay in front of Culainn's house with his huge head on his paws, ready to tear into pieces anyone who came there.

In Emain, the boys finished their play at last, and each went off to his parents' house. Setanta set off for Culainn's house, following the trail of the king's party. As he went he played with his ball, which he still carried with him.

As Setanta approached Culainn's house, the huge dog growled and stood up, his hair bristling, his teeth bared, ready to swallow in a single gulp the little child who came along playing with his ball. But Setanta was not afraid, even though he had no weapons and no means of defending himself. Thinking quickly, he threw his ball straight at the open mouth of the dog. As always, Setanta's aim was true, and the ball went straight into the dog's mouth. Before the dog could recover, Setanta grasped him by the hind legs and killed him.

Meanwhile, inside Culainn's house, through all the noise of the feasting and merry-making, Conchobar had heard the growling of the guard dog. 'Setanta!' cried Conchobar, remembering suddenly that he had asked the little boy to follow him to the feast. The king rose, and with him all his men, and rushed outside, fearing the worst. 'My sister's son has surely been torn to death by the hound,' grieved Conchobar.

But Setanta stood there, safe and sound. Fergus, one of Conchobar's trusted knights, lifted him on to his shoulder and carried him to the king, who was most relieved to see the child unharmed.

Then came Culainn the smith, who was most upset to see his guard dog lying dead. 'Welcome you are, little Setanta, for your mother and your father's sake,' said Culainn to the little boy. 'But I do not welcome you for your own sake. I wish I had never held this feast.'

'What do you have against the boy?' Conchobar asked Culainn, surprised at his ungracious words.

'My dog is dead,' said Culainn. 'He was the guardian of my wealth and my livelihood. Who now will look after my home and my wealth and my herds and protect me and mine? I am now a man bereft of livelihood.'

Then the boy Setanta spoke. 'Do not be angry, O Culainn,' said Setanta. 'If your dog has sired pups, bring to me the best of his pups and I will rear him and train him to make of him the best guard dog in all Erin (Ireland). And till he is grown, I myself will guard your home and your flocks and your cattle and even you, yourself.'

At this, Conchobar and all his men were greatly impressed. 'Well spoken, little fellow,' said Conchobar. 'I myself could not have given a better judgement than this.'

So Setanta took upon himself the duties of the hound of Culainn the smith.

'Let your name now be Cuchulainn, which means "wolfhound of Culainn",' said Cathba, the druid and seer who some said was Conchobar's natural father.

'Ah, no,' said Setanta. 'My own name, Setanta, son of Sualtim, is the one I prefer.'

'Ah, but Cuchulainn is the name that will make you famous,' said Cathba. 'In all of Erin and Alba (Scotland), men will hear that name and will speak it with wonder.' Cathba could foresee the future and so Setanta respected his prophecy.

'Then I will take the name that is being given to me,' said the little boy.

And Cuchulainn he became forever afterwards.

And Cathba spoke truly, for Cuchulainn was the name that resounded through all of Erin and Alba, then and forever afterwards.

How Cuchulainn Killed the Sons of Necht

One day, in Emain, Cathba the druid of King Conchobar, was taking classes in druidic lore. Eight eager students sat in his class, avidly taking in all that Cathba was teaching them. One of the eight then asked his teacher, 'O Cathba, can you tell us what fortune this day will bring? Will it be good or will it be ill?'

Cathba, druid and seer, then answered, 'The little boy who takes up arms today shall be renowned for deeds of arms above all the youths of Erin. The tales of his deeds shall be told forever. But his life will be short and fleeting.'

Seven-year-old Cuchulainn, at play in another corner of Emain, heard what Cathba said. At once, he threw his playthings away and ran to his uncle King Conchobar.

Conchobar saw the little boy come running up as though he had something very important to say. 'What is it, little fellow? It seems you have something to tell me,' asked Conchobar.

'I will take up arms today,' announced Cuchulainn to the king.

'Who has advised you to do so?' asked Conchobar.

'Cathba the druid has told me so,' said Cuchulainn.

'Cathba would not say wrong,' said Conchobar thoughtfully. And he gave to Cuchulainn two spears and a sword and a shield.

Cuchulainn took the spears and sword and shield and shook them, and they lay in fragments on the floor of Conchobar's hall.

Then Conchobar gave him another two spears, a sword and a shield. These too shattered into fragments in the little boy's hands.

Conchobar then gave him, one after another, all the weapons he had in reserve to arm the youths of Emain with. Cuchulainn took the weapons, one after another, and shook them, and all of them shattered into pieces one after another on the floor of Conchobar's hall.

'Truly, these arms are not good, O Conchobar,' said Cuchulainn. 'Give me weapons that are worthy of me!'

Then Conchobar gave the little boy his own two spears, his sword and his shield. Cuchulainn took the weapons and he brandished them in the air, and he shook them and bent them, and they did not break; they stood up to his strength and skill. 'These are good weapons, O Conchobar,' cried Cuchulainn. 'They suit me well.' And Cuchulainn saluted the weapons and the king to whom they belonged.

Just then, Cathba the druid came by. 'Has that child taken up arms?' he asked Conchobar, seeing Cuchulainn with spears and sword and shield.

'Yes,' answered Conchobar, 'he has.'

'Not for anything would I have had him take up arms this day!' cried Cathba.

'Why not?' asked Conchobar puzzled. 'Didn't you yourself advise him to do so?'

'Oh, no, I did not,' said Cathba.

Conchobar turned in anger to Cuchulainn. 'What is this I hear?' he asked. 'Did you trick us into giving you arms?'

'No, King, I did not,' answered Cuchulainn. 'Cathba did not speak directly to me, but he told his students that the boy who would take up arms today would be famous throughout Erin, though his life would be short and fleeting.'

'That is true,' agreed Cathba.

'Fortunate, I am, therefore,' said little Cuchulainn. 'What care I how short my life if my deeds be good and great and live after me!'

And when he was asked, Cathba also said, 'The one who mounts a chariot today, his deeds will live in Erin forever!'

Cuchulainn heard and tried out one chariot after another. Not one of the chariots that Conchobar had reserved for the youths of Emain stood up to little Cuchulainn, but broke instead into a hundred pieces.

Then Conchobar called to Ibar his charioteer and said, 'Take my own two horses and yoke them to my chariot and give them to the child.'

Ibar did as he was asked, and Cuchulainn mounted the chariot of Conchobar and it withstood his strength and did not break. 'Truly, this is a good chariot, O King,' cried Cuchulainn. 'It is suited to me.'

'Come now, little boy,' said Ibar, after Cuchulainn had tried out the chariot. 'Get down from the chariot, and let the horses out to graze.'

'It is too soon,' said Cuchulainn. 'Let me take first a round of Emain, since this is my first day of taking up arms.' And Cuchulainn set off on a round of Emain.

Then Ibar said once again, 'Come now, little boy. Get down from the chariot and let the horses out to graze.'

And Cuchulainn said, 'It is still too soon. Let me drive

as far as the fields where the boys are playing, so that they may wish me well on my first day of taking up arms.' And Cuchulainn drove out to the playing fields of Emain.

The boys saw Cuchulainn with arms, riding his chariot and wished him victory, triumph and first wounding. 'But it is too soon for you to take up arms,' they said. 'You will no longer play with us!'

'Oh, no,' said Cuchulainn. 'I will not leave you. It is only for luck that I took up arms today.'

Then Ibar said yet again, 'Come now, little boy. Get down from the chariot and let the horses out to graze.'

But Cuchulainn answered yet again that it was too soon, for he wanted to follow the road that wound so invitingly before them.

Cuchulainn followed the road, which led up into the mountains. On the border of Ulster, there stood a watchman—Connall Cernach, it was that day, who stood watch, to make sure no unwanted strangers entered Ulster.

When Connall saw Cuchulainn come driving by in Conchobar's chariot and with his weapons, he asked, 'Has the little fellow taken up arms?'

'Yes, indeed, he has,' said Ibar.

The Connell wished Cuchulainn victory, but cautioned him, 'You're too young to take up arms, little boy, for you are not yet old enough to do great deeds.'

But Cuchulainn was eager to try out his new weapons. Perhaps he could do so defending the border, he thought. 'Let me keep watch in your place, O Connell,' he said.

But Connell wouldn't hear of it. 'Ah, no, little boy, I couldn't do that,' said Connell. 'You are still too young to take on a real warrior should one appear to challenge you.'

'Well, then,' said Cuchulainn. 'I shall carry on to the south. Perhaps there I will find a chance to use my weapons.'

When Connell saw that the child was determined, he said, 'I cannot let you go into danger alone on the border. If something were to happen to you, no one would forgive me, saying I let a child go alone into danger. I will come with you.' So Connell yoked his horses to his chariot and followed Cuchulainn, in order to protect the child.

Cuchulainn saw that Connell would not let him go alone. 'He will not let me try my weapons even if I had the chance,' thought Cuchulainn. Taking a stone and fixing it into his sling, Cuchulainn threw the stone at Connell's chariot, so that the yoke broke and Connell was thrown to the ground.

'What is this, little fellow?' cried Connell. 'Why did you throw that stone at me?'

'I do not want you to follow me,' said Cuchulainn. 'And the only way to stop you was to break your chariot, for I know that it is forbidden among you men of Ulster to continue on a journey if your chariot has an accident of any sort.'

Connell admitted the truth of that, and leaving Cuchulainn to carry on southwards, turned back to his post.

Cuchulainn carried on, in search of a chance to try his weapons. Time and again, Ibar would urge him to turn back, for it was late and it was time they returned, but each time Cuchulainn found a reason to carry on.

Then, Cuchulainn saw a fort in the distance. 'What is that fort, O Ibar?' he asked.

'That is the fort of the three sons of Necht Scene the Fierce. Foill and Fandall and Tuachall are their names. Their father was slain by an Ulsterman, and they hate all men of Ulster since.'

'Are they the ones who boast that they have killed more Ulstermen than are alive?' asked Cuchulainn.

'Alas, yes,' said Ibar. 'They are the ones—and they are dangerous.'

'Onwards, then!' cried Cuchulainn.

Disregarding all Ibar's protests, Cuchulainn drove on to the fort of the sons of Necht. There, on the green, stood a stone with an iron band around it and with writing on it in Ogham. This is what the writing said: 'Whoever comes to the green, if he be a champion, he cannot leave without giving challenge to single combat.' Cuchulainn read the writing, and taking up the stone threw it, iron band and all, so that it fell into the river and sank.

'Ah,' sighed Ibar. 'I think that on this green you will finally get the chance you are seeking, to try your new weapons and prove yourself.'

'Good,' said Cuchulainn, and not in the least worried, he asked Ibar to spread the skins for him so that he may have a nap. Ibar did as he asked, and the child lay down to sleep.

Just then, out came Foill, son of Necht, on to the green. 'Whose are these horses?' he demanded.

'Conchobar's,' answered Ibar and explained how a lad who was but a child had driven them out that day, the day that he had taken up arms for good luck.

'May his taking up of arms be not for victory,' cried Foill. 'If I knew that he were old enough to fight, he would not leave here alive.'

'Ah, he is not old enough,' said Ibar. 'He is only a child of seven, even though he has taken up arms today.'

At that, Cuchulainn woke up, and declared angrily that he was as fit as any warrior to fight.

Cuchulainn armed himself, as did Foill. Foill, who, it was said, could not be harmed by point or sharpened edge, advanced on the little child. But before Foill could strike, Cuchulainn threw his staff at him and killed him. Then he cut off Foill's head and carried it off with him.

Just then, out came Tuachall, the second son of Necht. When he saw that Cuchulainn had killed his brother, he swore that the boy would not leave the green alive. Ibar warned Cuchulainn to beware, for if Tuachall escaped the first blow, he could not be defeated. But before Tuachall could attack, Cuchulainn ran him through the chest with Conchobar's lance. Then he cut off Tuachall's head and laid it beside that of his brother.

Just then, out came Fandall, youngest son of Necht. 'Fools, my brothers were, to fight you on dry land,' he cried. 'Come with me to the pool and fight me there, and you shall not leave here alive.'

'Be careful, little lad,' Ibar warned Cuchulainn. 'Fandall

is the best swimmer in the world, and no one can beat him in the water.'

'You should not worry about me,' said little Cuchulainn to Ibar. 'In Emain, when the boys play in the river and some of them grow tired, I carry them across, a boy on each palm of my hand, and one on each shoulder, and I do not even wet my ankles with their weight.'

So Cuchulainn went down to the pool to fight Fandall. The two wrestled on the surface of the water, and Cuchulainn gripped Fandall, and cut off his head with Conchobar's sword and carried it off to lay it with the heads of his brothers.

After that, Cuchulainn destroyed the fort of the sons of Necht and burnt it down to the ground. He then took the heads of the three sons of Necht and turned back towards Emain.

On the way, he saw a herd of wild deer in the distance. 'Let us try and catch some,' cried Cuchulainn. But though Ibar drove the horses as fast as they could go, they were not fleet enough to catch the deer. So Cuchulainn dismounted from the chariot, and easily caught two of the swift, fierce deer. He tied them to the chariot and continued on his way to Emain.

After a while, they saw a flock of swans flying by. 'What birds are those, O Ibar?' asked Cuchulainn. Ibar explained that they were swans, and that came from the rocks and crags of the sea to feed on the plains of Emain.

'What is a greater deed, O Ibar?' asked Cuchulainn. 'To take them alive or to take them dead?'

Ibar explained that it was definitely a greater feat to take the swans alive, for though many men had taken them dead, few had ever taken the great birds alive.

So Cuchulainn fitted a stone into his sling and brought down eight of them. Then he fitted another stone on his sling and brought down sixteen of them. As the birds lay stunned on the ground, Cuchulainn asked Ibar to get down from the chariot and gather them.

'I dare not move,' said Ibar. 'I cannot control the horses any more, and if I move from where I am, the horses will go wild and I will be crushed under the chariot wheels. And if I so much as stir from where I am, the horns of the deer will gore me.'

Then Cuchulainn bent upon the horses a fierce glare, and also upon the deer. The horses stayed still and the deer bowed their heads in fear, so that Ibar could gather up the great white birds that Cuchulainn had brought down. Then they tied the birds to the chariot and went on their way to Emain.

As they neared Emain, the fearsome chariot with its marvellous load of grisly heads and pinioned deer and white swans still alive was seen. 'It is my sister's son who comes thus,' cried Conchobar when he was told of the sight. 'The battle frenzy is still upon him, and unless he is cooled, all the sons of Emain will die by his hand tonight.'

At this, the women of Emain ran out to meet him, and as they neared the child they bared their bodies. Cuchulainn did not know what to do when he saw the women thus. He averted his eyes and looked only at his chariot. And while he was thus looking away, the little boy was lifted down from the chariot and put into three vats of cold water to cool his wrath. The first vat into which he was put burst with the heat of his battle frenzy. The second vat into which he was put boiled with bubbles as big as a man's fist. The third vat into which he was put—well, some men might be able to bear it, and some men not. Then the boy's anger left him, and he was taken out and dressed in his best clothes.

Then the little lad Cuchulainn was seated in the place of honour, between the two feet of Conchobar. That became his place forever, and everyone gazed in wonder at this little boy of seven who had taken up arms that very day and overcome three fearsome warriors at whose hands had fallen two-thirds of the men of Ulster.

Thus it was that Cuchulainn took up arms and killed on the same day the sons of Necht. Cathba the druid had spoken truly, for still are the deeds of Cuchulainn sung, in Erin and all the world. And truly too did Cathba prophesy that Cuchulainn's life would be short and fleeting, for Cuchulainn died long before he had lived to the full age of mortal men—but that is another tale, for another day.

Twenty-Four Bends in the Min River

Most of our knowledge of ancient Chinese myths comes from books which have been copied and re-copied by generations of scribes over thousands of years.

In Chinese myth, as well as in China today, dragons represent power, wisdom and intelligence. In this story, the little boy, who is hardworking, wise and kind, turns into a dragon—which is always considered to be a creature on a plane higher than the merely human.

In south-west China, through the province of Sichuan, there flows the wild and beautiful Min River. It is said that long ago the river ran straight and true, from its source in the Min Mountains to the point where it flowed into the great Yangtze River and became one with it. But today, the river twists and turns on itself twenty-four times, as though in anguish too great to be borne, and within each of the twenty-four bends of the river there nestles a small lake, almost like a teardrop. People who live along the Min River tell a strange story about a little boy who made the bends in the river and caused the lakes to form.

Long ago, in a little village by the Min River, there lived a little boy called Wen P'eng and his widowed mother.

In the same village, in the biggest and grandest house, there lived a rich and cruel man. This man owned all the land for miles around, and made all the poor people of the village work in his fields for little more than a handful of rice every year. In addition to being very rich, this man was cruel and wicked as well. He would punish ruthlessly, and sometimes even kill, any person who disobeyed him. Everyone in the village was terrified of him. They began to call him 'Black Tiger' because of his evil and vicious ways.

Wen P'eng's father had been killed by Black Tiger a few years ago, and now the boy and his mother were very poor. Wen P'eng was still too young to work in the fields, so he would go fishing every day. He would sell the fish he caught in the village, and he and his mother survived on the few coins he would thus earn.

On some days it would happen that Wen P'eng would sit by the river from dawn to dusk, and still catch nothing. On such days he and his mother would go to bed hungry.

One day, Wen P'eng had been sitting by the river all day and had not caught a single fish. It began to grow dark, and the little boy decided to go home. Just then he felt a pull at his line. Wen P'eng tried to draw in his line, but he couldn't. He pulled and he pulled with all his strength, and just as he was on the point of giving up, out came the fish.

It was the most beautiful fish he had ever seen. Its scales were made of purest gold, that gleamed and glittered so brightly that Wen P'eng had to shut his eyes against the dazzle. 'This fish should fetch a good price in the village,' said Wen P'eng aloud, pleased that tonight he would be able to take home extra money for his mother. But just then the fish wriggled its tail and began speaking in a human voice.

'Wen P'eng,' said the fish. 'Please do not kill me. Let me go and I will reward you richly.'

Wen P'eng looked at the fish hanging at the end of his line and sighed. 'I couldn't kill such a beautiful creature,' he thought, and he threw the fish back into the water. Sadly, the little boy began to wind up his line, knowing that once again he and his mother would have nothing to eat that night.

But suddenly, the fish raised its head above the water, and swimming to the riverbank, dropped a large pearl at the boy's feet and said, 'Take good care of this pearl Wen

P'eng, and from now you shall have plenty of everything.' Before Wen P'eng could say a word, the fish vanished into the river.

Wen P'eng took the pearl home and gave it to his mother. 'Oh, dear Wen P'eng,' cried his mother in despair. 'What are we going to do with this pearl? We cannot eat it, and if we try to sell it, people will think we stole it.' In fear and frustration, his mother threw the pearl into a corner of the room. The pearl fell into the rice bin, in which there remained a few grains of rice.

'We have nothing to eat tonight, my son,' wept Wen P'eng's mother. 'It would have been better had you sold the golden fish. At least I could have bought some rice to feed you with.' The woman rose and went to the rice bin to scrape together the few grains of rice that remained. 'Perhaps I can cook them into a broth for my boy,' she thought. But instead of the empty bin, what did she see? The bin was full to the top with fine white rice and overflowing with it!

'Wen P'eng,' cried the mother in excitement. 'I think your pearl is magic!' And she picked up the pearl and put it into her little sack of money, which contained only a few copper coins. All at once, the bag began to fill with money, till it was full to the top with shining coins.

Now Wen P'eng and his mother had plenty of everything and lacked for nothing. But Wen P'eng continued to work as hard as before and would go fishing every day just as he used to.

One day, while Wen P'eng was away by the river, Black Tiger's wife came to pay a visit to his mother. Black Tiger's wife was as cruel and as greedy as her husband. She had noticed that Wen P'eng and his mother no longer looked as though they were starving, and that they had new clothes to wear and money to spend in the market. She wanted to know the source of their well-being, and had come to find out.

'I know that you and your son are thieves,' said Black Tiger's wife to Wen P'eng's mother.

'Of course not,' cried Wen P'eng's mother in horror. 'My son and I are honest people! We've never taken anything that doesn't belong to us!'

'Well, then, how do you explain the fact that suddenly you seem to have enough food to eat and new clothes to wear and money to spend in the market? Till yesterday you were starving!'

Wen P'eng's mother looked worried. 'We've just been fortunate,' she said. She did not want to tell Black Tiger's wife the truth, but she was frightened of being called a thief.

'Fortunate! What nonsense!' cried Black Tiger's wife. 'Since when is a peasant fortunate? You are a thief, and so is that precious son of yours, and I will make sure that my husband hears all about it!'

'Oh no, please, not that!' cried Wen P'eng's mother in fright. 'Please don't say anything to your husband. I will tell you the truth.' And the poor, frightened woman poured out the entire story of the fish and the magic pearl to Black Tiger's wife.

Black Tiger's wife listened amazed. 'I must have that pearl!' she thought to herself. And off she ran to her husband and told him the whole story.

Meanwhile, Wen P'eng returned home after the day's fishing. He found his mother weeping. 'Oh, my son,' cried the woman. 'We are undone! Black Tiger's wife knows our secret and I'm afraid her husband will soon be here to demand our pearl!'

Wen P'eng turned pale with worry.

Just then there was a loud hammering on the door. The Black Tiger and his bailiffs stood outside.

'Give me the pearl!' commanded Black Tiger. 'Peasants like you have no right to own such a magical thing!' But Wen P'eng stood still and silent, and his mother wept tears of worry and fright.

'Search the house!' then ordered Black Tiger. His men turned the house upside down but they could not find the pearl. And all the while Wen P'eng stood still and silent, and his mother wept tears of worry and fright.

'Where have you hidden the pearl?' growled Black Tiger, taking Wen P'eng by the throat and shaking him hard. 'Answer, or I shall drag you before the judge and call you a thief to all the world!' But Wen P'eng said not a word.

At last, Black Tiger left, cursing and threatening.

Wen P'eng's mother ran to her son who still stood silent, but with a most peculiar expression on his face.

'Oh, Wen P'eng,' she cried. 'What is wrong with you? You have such a strange look on your face!'

'Oh, Mother,' gasped Wen P'eng. 'I was holding the pearl in my mouth and I swallowed it when Black Tiger shook me! I cannot breathe and my heart is beating as though it would burst!'

'Oh, my child,' cried the mother. 'What can I do to help you? That pearl was magic—goodness knows what effect it will have on you!'

And Wen P'eng answered, 'Oh, Mother, give me some water. I am terribly thirsty.'

The mother ran and fetched him some water. But Wen P'eng cried, 'This thirst is terrible. I cannot bear it. I must go down to the river.' The boy turned and ran towards the river, his mother running after him and weeping as she ran.

Wen P'eng reached the river, and flinging himself into the water drank and drank, till the river was almost empty. Suddenly, the sky became overcast, lightning flashed, thunder rolled and a sharp wind began to blow.

Wen P'eng's mother looked at her son, and screamed in fear—there, before her eyes, her beloved son was slowly turning into a dragon!

'My son! My child!' shrieked the woman, and jumping into the river, grabbed Wen P'eng by his foot. But she could not stop the pearl's magic. Her son turned into a dragon, all except for one foot, the foot that she had been holding.

'I must go, Mother,' whispered the dragon sadly. 'I cannot stay with you any longer.'

'Don't leave me, my child,' wept the mother. 'I cannot live without you!'

'I cannot help it, Mother,' sighed the dragon. 'Something more powerful than me is pulling me away from you!'

Slowly, the dragon rose into the air, his great wings outspread, the scales on his body shining gold and red.

'Look back at me, my son!' called the woman. 'Look at me once more before you go!'

The dragon heard his mother and looked back, twisting and turning his great body in anguish, and a tear rolled from his eye and fell beside the river.

'My son, look back once more!' begged the woman.

The dragon looked back again and one more tear dropped from his eye beside the river.

Twenty-four times did the mother call to her son to look back, and twenty-four times did the dragon turn around, twisting and turning, in torment with the pain of parting, dropping twenty-four tears beside the river.

And that is why, people say, the Min River twists and turns on itself twenty-four times, as though in anguish too great to be borne, and which is why within each bend of the river there nestles a lake, like a teardrop.

Benkei and Yoshitsune

Benkei was a warrior monk who lived in Japan in the twelfth century. Though stories about him are exaggerated into mythic proportions, he was undoubtedly a real person.

Minamoto Yoshitsune is one of the best-loved historical figures in Japan. He was a brilliant warrior who lived from 1159 to 1189. He helped his older brother Yoritomo gain control of Japan. Later, Yoritomo established the first shogunate in Japan.

Yoshitsune's father, Minamoto Yoshihomo was killed by his enemy Taira Kiyomori in 1160, when Yoshitsune was less than a year old. Kiyomori spared Yoshitsune, but put him in a monastery in Kyoto. Here, Yoshitsune trained to become a Buddhist monk.

Legend says that it was near this monastery, on the Goyo Bridge in Kyoto that Yoshitsune met Benkei.

Yoshitsune and Benkei remain among Japan's best-loved heroes. Their adventures have given birth to a host of myths, legends and stories, while incidents from their lives often form the theme of Kabuki plays and Noh performances.

Nine hundred years ago, in Japan, a blacksmith's daughter gave birth to a baby boy. Some said the boy's father was a god, but most said his father was an evil spirit. But one thing everyone agreed on—that the baby was different from other human children. He was an unusually large baby, and had been born with long hair like a wild man's, and big sharp teeth. He had the strength of twelve men, and he grew far more rapidly than other babies did. Soon everyone began calling him Oniwaka, which means 'devil's child'.

As a little boy, Oniwaka was always getting into trouble, fighting this child or that, breaking this thing or that. His poor mother was driven mad dealing with her neighbour's complaints and trying to keep the child in check. At last, at her wits' end, she decided to send him into a monastery. Living in the quiet atmosphere there with only serene and disciplined men for company would calm his rowdy spirit, she thought.

So little Oniwaka became a monk. But even so he kept

getting into trouble, and being sent from one monastery to another, from one temple to another, in the hope that somewhere he would settle down.

Finally, when he was seventeen years old, Oniwaka left the monasteries and became a *Yamabushi*, a wandering, bandit monk. He began calling himself Saito Musashibo Benkei.

Benkei was a huge man, almost two metres tall, and with supernatural strength. He took great pride in his skill with arms, and would often challenge unsuspecting travellers to a fight, on the condition that whoever won the fight would also win his opponent's sword. Of course, Benkei never lost a single fight, and at the end of just a few years, he had collected nine hundred and ninety-nine swords. He was now in search of his thousandth sword.

One day, Benkei wished to offer special evening prayers at the Kitano shrine in Kyoto. But other monks warned him, 'Do not go to Kitano, Benkei. A spirit guards the Goyo Bridge, which you will have to cross on your way.'

'I am not afraid of a spirit,' said Benkei amused.

'Ah, no, Benkei. We know you are not afraid of anything. But this spirit even Benkei should beware! It kills all those who dare cross Goyo Bridge after dark.'

Now, more than ever, Benkei was determined to offer evening prayers at Kitano shrine. 'Perhaps I will win my one-thousandth sword fighting this spirit,' said Benkei to himself.

As he approached Goyo Bridge, all was quiet and very

dark. There was no one in sight. Then, just as Benkei was about to cross the bridge, there jumped before him the figure of a little boy.

'Ah, the spirit,' thought Benkei to himself. He bowed low before the spirit and said, 'Let me pass. I go to offer evening prayers at Kitano shrine.'

But the spirit spoke up in the voice of a young boy and cried, 'Stand and fight! If you defeat me, you may pass, else not!'

Benkei accepted the challenge, and drawing his sword, faced the spirit. Benkei had never faced such an opponent in his life. The spirit leaped and danced and parried and thrust as though he had wings. Soon Benkei was fighting to retain his position, and then he was fighting for his life! And suddenly the fight was over, with Benkei at the spirit's mercy and acknowledging defeat.

'You are a good swordsman,' said the spirit, 'so I will spare your life.'

Benkei bowed low before him. 'Who are you?' he asked. 'In all my life I have never met anyone—mortal or spirit—who could beat me.'

The spirit answered, 'My name is Ushiwaka. I am the son of Minamoto Yoshihomo, and younger brother of Yoritomo!'

'You are no spirit then!' cried Benkei.

'Ah no,' laughed Ushiwaka. 'I am as mortal as anyone else!'

Benkei looked in wonder at this young boy, little more

than ten years old, who had so effortlessly defeated him. And Benkei bowed his head before him and humbly asked to serve him for the rest of his life. Ushiwaka accepted Benkei as his follower.

When Ushiwaka grew up, he was known as Yoshitsune. Benkei never left Yoshitsune's side, and died in battle minutes after Yoshitsune. The spirits of Benkei and Yoshitsune left their bodies at the same time, and some say they are still together.

The deeds of Yoshitsune, the great warrior, and his faithful follower Benkei are still remembered in Japan.